MONSTER
WHITE
LIES

BY KIMBERLY ANN FREEL

*Warm Regards —
Kimberly Ann Freel*

Country Messenger Press Publishing Group, LLC
Okanogan, Washington

All inquiries should be addressed to:

CMPPG, LLC
27657 Highway 97
Okanogan, WA 98840

Monster White Lies may be ordered from CMPPG, LLC at the above address and at **cmppg.com**

Monster White Lies is also available at **Amazon.com**.

Contact Publisher for distributor information.

email: **cmppg@cmppg.com**
website: **cmppg.com**

ISBN:0-9619407-4-3
ISBN13: 978-0-9619407-4-4

To Mom. You once said I could be anything I wanted to be, and do anything I wanted to do. I believe you now as much as I did then.

What a lucky kid I was to have a mom like you. I love you.

PROLOGUE

Lillian pressed herself closer to the wall of the hall closet, breathing shallowly to avoid discovery, trying desperately to process what she knew, the stale air stifling her.

She had seen the girl first: the one from the hospital, the candy striper. She was padding around the house in her bare feet, stringy blond hair hanging limp, eyes vacant. She had a baby bottle in her hand and was shaking it absently, leaving spots of formula down her baggy muslin dress.

Lillian had come in through the back door, intent on investigating the goings-on in her sister's house. She had house-sat for Dev and Shannon when they went on their last trip to Tahiti, about six months before Beatrice was born. That had left her with a key to the back door of their St. Louis brick home and she had kept it in case of an emergency, which this was. Shannon had never gone so long without calling.

The last time they talked, they had, as they always did, discussed the rumors at the hospital. St. Louis State Hospital was a mental institution and stories about the wacky patients abounded, but, like most hospitals, nothing turned quite as efficiently as the rumor mill. Lillian was a registered nurse at the hospital. Shannon was married to one of its most famous psychiatrists, Milton "Dev" Devon, Jr.

The latest gossip had been that one of the candy-

iv

stripers was pregnant and was blabbing all around the hospital that the father of her baby was a *doctor*. The girl was barely eighteen, her long blond hair always pulled neatly back into a thick braid. She had braces and a lisp because of them. She was young and acted like it in all the ways that counted. But, as Lillian told Shannon, her little pink and white outfit was beginning to look rather ridiculous with her bulging belly. It was obvious that she was, indeed, pregnant.

They had talked about other things in the cafeteria during that lunch hour. Like Lillian's favorite patient, Hugh Q., who kept propositioning her, naked, when she entered his padded room to give him his daily meds. They talked about Beatrice, who was cute as a button and growing like a weed. She had been starting to walk, intermittently, and getting into *everything*.

Shannon talked about her postpartum depression, which she was finally starting to work past. Dev made sure she was properly medicated. She worked on getting fit again and spending a few precious hours every week away from her active baby girl, with the help of a part-time nanny. Shannon seemed happier, back on track, better than she had been in months, in Lillian's experienced opinion.

But that had been three months ago. She and her younger sister had never gone three months without talking. She was worried about Shannon. Dev had been vague when Lillian inquired about her. Lillian had never trusted him, but he did seem to love her sister. When he wouldn't give her a straight answer, Lillian decided that, on her day off, she would investigate on her own.

Lillian followed candy-striper girl quietly. She struggled to remember her name, but before she could, the girl took a quick right into Dev's office. Lillian went past the door and then hid herself around the door jam as she peered inside. The inside of the dark-paneled office looked amazingly different. There were blue curtains on the windows, an eyelet-lined crib and changing table in front of the massive desk. Most amazing of all was the squall that came from the hungry infant in the bowels of the crib.

Why would that girl have her baby in this house?

Before she could wonder any longer, the girl rushed out of the office, still looking and acting like an automaton. She didn't even see Lillian pressed against the wall outside the doorway. Lillian went quickly inside the office and peeked at the infant, whose bottle had been propped on a pillow next to him. He was sucking his breakfast greedily, his eyes open, his arms raised, fists gripping and ungripping as he tried to soothe his hungry tummy.

The girl, whatever her name was, wasn't a very good mommy leaving this poor guy here to drink his bottle all by himself. Lillian quietly closed the door of the office and scooped up the baby boy and his bottle and held him in Dev's office chair while he consumed it. It gave her a chance to study him.

He was bald, but tiny baby hairs were starting at the crown of his head. It was clear that he would be quite blond. His eyes, though, were startlingly dark. They still had a tinge of baby blue, but they were changing toward a more muddy color. Lillian had not seen a whole lot of babies at this age, so it could have been her limited experience, but she thought this guy looked an awful lot like her niece, Beatrice. His face was a little rounder, but through the eyes, they looked surprisingly similar.

It dawned on Lillian all at once the reason why this

baby boy would be in Dev's office. Beatrice didn't look anything like Shannon. She looked just like her dad. And so did this baby boy.

Lillian's calm burst into flames when she realized that the doctor that fathered the candy-striper's baby was Dr. Dev Devon himself. How could he have *slept* with such a young girl in the first place? What in the world were the mother and baby doing in this house anyway? Wouldn't you think that he would try to hide them somewhere else? Now Lillian was doubly worried about the welfare of her sister.

The baby fell asleep while drinking his bottle, so Lillian place him gently back into his crib and slipped quietly back into the hallway.

She heard voices from the downstair's guest bedroom.

"Did you feed Benjamin this morning, Diana?"

"Oh, yeah, 'Diana' was her name," Lillian thought silently.

"Yes, Dev, I gave him a bottle, just like you showed me. I left it for him in his crib."

"You must hold him while he's eating, Diana. It's much better for his development and that way he can't choke."

"I know. You told me that, but I'm tired this morning," she started to whine. "He was up all night, asking to be fed. He's *your* son too. Why don't *you* feed him once in a while?"

"But you are his mother. I have other things to take care of. Don't you forget, sweetheart, what your situation is here."

Dev's voice was like ice. He had always been conceited, arrogant, and barely civil to his wife's sister.

Lillian never had much use for Dr. Dev Devon. He was a jerk, but when had he become such a monster?

"I expect you to take care of Benjamin, Diana. The nanny will continue to see to Beatrice. I will keep a roof over all of your heads. Now, you be a good girl while I go give my son a kiss."

"Can you change his diaper, while you're there?" Diana was whining again.

"Very well," Dev sighed. Lillian concealed herself in the darkened hall bathroom as he strode toward the nursery office.

She stole up the entryway staircase to her sister's room. It was locked and she didn't hear anyone inside. She did, however, hear Dev close his office door and head for the stairs. She ran quickly to Beatrice's nursery across the hall. The shade was pulled and it was dark, so she was able to observe her sister's room through the crack of the door. Dev entered the silent bedroom.

Then Lillian heard her sister's plea. "Don't leave me again, Dev. I need to see her. Please. I'm begging you." Then she had heard a pitiful, helpless moan, followed by eery silence. Was he killing her? Oh, God. What was happening to her sister inside that room?

She was pretty sure that Dev didn't see her or hear her barely audible gasp when she watched him leave her sister's room and lock the door with a shiny key ring.

She had run for the downstairs hall closet while Dev returned to his suite, presumably to get ready for work. She would wait until he left and get to the bottom of this.

Why did it have to be so muggy this time of year? And why did she have to wind up in the only place in the house that didn't have a fan?

Her honey-colored hair was plastered to her head and she was miserably sweaty, anxious to breathe real air as soon as possible. She heard the front door open and close. Assuming that Dev had left, Lillian waited ten unbearable minutes then stole away from her hiding place and back up the stairs. The baby was squalling again. No time for that. His whiny mother could see to him.

Lillian knocked gently at her sister's door. "Shan, it's me. Are you still there?" She pleaded, hoping against hope that her sister would be able to hear her.

Shannon's voice was garbled, muffled by the locked door. Lillian could barely make out what she was saying. One word was clear, though. "Beatrice."

"Shannon, honey, how can I help you? Please, you need to tell me."

"No help me," her sister mumbled. It sounded like she was now just behind the door, near the floor, like she had drug herself there.

Lillian fumbled with the door lock, to no avail. "Shannon, please tell me what to do."

"Get Beatrice. Take her."

"Where is she, Shan? I haven't seen her here today."

"So tired......" Shannon's voice trailed off.

Lillian had a ton of experience extracting information from sedated patients. She put on her most authoritative nurse's voice. "Shannon. Be sharp. You must tell me what you want for Beatrice."

"At the park. With her nanny. Take her. Go away."

Shannon and Lillian often took Beatrice for walks to Forest Park. It was their favorite place in the city because of the magnificent centuries old trees, the serene ponds, and the zoo animals. She hoped this was the park Shannon was referring to.

"I'll find her, Shannon. Are you sure you want me to take her? Where should I take her?"

"Away from him. Never come back, Lilly," Shannon was sounding progressively clearer. Lillian knew what she had to do. Dr. Dev Devon had crossed nearly every line and he was getting away with it. Her sister wanted her to take Beatrice, his precious daughter, away from him. She would do it. For Shannon, she would do just about anything. Her little sister was the only family she had left.

"I love you, Shan." Lillian's tears flowed freely as she knew she was saying goodbye to her little sister forever. But she also knew that she needed to get out of this house before she was discovered. "I want to help you, desperately. Are you sure this is the only way?"

"Go, Lilly. Only way. So tired……Can't." Shannon was fading again. Lillian tore herself wretchedly away and left quickly out the back door to find her niece.

CHAPTER ONE

The sun was shining and the glistening water of the Columbia River beckoned. BreeAnn White and Nonnie Pakootas were about to brave their first late spring dip into its frigid waters. They had both worn swimsuits in anticipation of an unseasonably warm day—it was supposed to be as much as 90 degrees by mid-afternoon. Over the top of their swimsuits, however, they had on t-shirts and their "Nannies" mascot sweatpants.

Neither of them had any illusions about this first swim. They had been doing this since they were ten. Bree and Nonnie knew by now that it would take about ten minutes treading water off the docks of the waterfront before their skinny bodies would start to stiffen and their lips would turn blue. They needed something warm and dry to fend off the cold when they dragged themselves out of the water.

Their mothers failed to understand why the two of them insisted on this annual ritual, but they had left the bakery to supervise the adventure for eight straight years now. The understanding was that the weather had to reach 90 degrees before the girls were allowed to Popsicle-ize themselves. And if both moms hadn't been decked out in flour-stained aprons and matching hair covers, they might have been tempted to join their daughters.

The River Run Bakery was across the street from the waterfront park in an old grocery store. Lilly White had moved it there nine years earlier after the bakery's

1

success had necessitated a larger space and easier access for distribution of their delicious baked goods. Merchants and customers flocked from all over Okanogan County to get a load of the oozing sticky buns and goody-packed cookies and loaves of "Mile-High Honey Wheat Bread."

Lilly attributed a good portion of the bakery's success to her faithful assistant, Penny Pakootas. With Lilly's swift business sense and lofty quality standards and Penny's uncanny ability to make yeast and flour do her bidding, the bakery was easily the largest in the county. They were a great team. It also helped that their daughters were inseparable.

Lilly, formerly Lillian Waters, rarely thought of the tumultuous beginning of her sojourn in Pateros. She had been on the run with Beatrice. They had settled so thoroughly into their lives here that she hardly thought of the exhausted fugitive and travel-weary baby that had arrived sixteen years before.

It seemed like nowadays, Lilly and Penny were spending a lot of their spare time reminiscing, getting misty-eyed as they recalled the mischief and fun the girls had cultivated over the years. The girls were about to graduate and neither mom was ready.

But the girls were more than ready. Bree was busily working on her valedictorian address. She had just two more weeks to prepare and, true to form, she was going to be perfect. It was her last chance, after all, to address the fifteen other seniors with whom she'd shared an idyllic childhood in the tiny town of Pateros, Washington. She was going to miss them, but at the same time her pulse thrummed every time she thought of the adventures awaiting her at the University of Washington and its

Journalism department.

Bree couldn't wait to take on Seattle. She'd always been such a big fish in this little pond. She wanted to see what it was like to be a small fish in a large pond for once. She didn't want so much to be anonymous, just individual—acting like herself instead of like the overachiever her classmates and her mom had always expected her to be.

Nonnie was anxious for graduation also, but not for the same reasons as Bree. Nonnie couldn't wait to be done with school. She had always struggled academically. She wasn't stupid, not by a long shot. People always commented that Nonnie was Bree's common sense. Bree was book-smart. Nonnie was street-smart. Unfortunately, though, she had dyslexia, so reading was a struggle and it always would be. She was looking forward to leaving the books behind for a while.

Now and again, Nonnie got a little wistful about graduating simply because her summer vacations were about to disappear. She had inherited her mother's talent for baking and she was going to a culinary school in California in the fall that would last for just three months. After that, Nonnie would be working full-time. This was her last chance to be carefree for the summer and she was going to make it count.

She was the first to rid herself of her overclothes. "Last one in is a stinky, wet dog!"

Bree giggled and hurried to shed her tennis shoes, knowing Nonnie had a decent head start, "First one in is a sticky, icky, river-gunk-covered icicle!"

"Yeah, well, taste my splash, puppy!"

By now, Bree was in hysterics. The darn shoelaces

wouldn't come undone and she couldn't for the life of her get them to just slip off her heels. Why did she double-knot those suckers?

Before she knew it, Nonnie was shrieking at the sudden iciness of the river. "Wait up, Nonnie! I can't get off my friggin' shoes!"

"Well you better hurry up," Nonnie gasped, "I just got in and I already can't feel my toes!"

"So much to look forward to! Maybe I'll just stay in my cozy, dry outfit."

"No way, Chickadee," piped in Lilly, calling Bree her favorite nickname, "Penny and I had a bet as to who would stay in the longest. I'm not rolling out the sticky buns in the morning. My muscles couldn't take it. Now get in there and freeze that skinny little rump, missy."

Bree was finally getting the knots of her shoelaces undone and rushing to discard her sweats and shirt. "I got it handled, Mom. Don't you worry about those muscles."

"B-b-b-ig M-m-m-istake, L-l-l-illy," Nonnie stuttered, "Y-y-you kn-know m-my Ind-ian f-f-fat insulates m-me."

Penny calmly started Bree's stopwatch as she dove headlong into the frigid water. "You go, Nonnie-girl."

To Lilly she said, "Like that girl's got any fat. Now me," she said as she measured her ample waist, "I could do some serious spring swimming with all the insulation I have."

"You and me both," Lilly giggled.

They watched as the girls gritted their teeth and treaded water. Soon it was Bree who had to drag herself out first as her limbs threatened to stop moving entirely. Lilly was ready with the towel. Nonnie was right behind her and Penny swallowed her into a towel and a large bear hug.

"So how was it, girls. Good as ever?" Penny inquired.

"All I know is that spring will never be the same if we don't arrange to do this again next year," Bree lamented.

All four of the women got momentarily choked up as they thought of the changes coming. If they could freeze time as easily as their young bodies, Bree and Nonnie would.

But growing up was inevitable.

Take today for instance. After their traditional swim, their mothers had given the girls consent to go on their first independent shopping trip to Wenatchee. It was just an hour's drive to the South, but it was going to be dark before they returned, so this really was a first—neither mom would be going with them.

The girls needed dresses and accessories to go under their graduation gowns. They were giddy as they changed from their wet clothes at Nonnie's house. Nonnie was going to drive her car. They were going to see an afternoon movie and have lunch at *Applebaum's* and then they were going to shop, leaving no stone unturned until they were fully decked out.

Nonnie's car was an old compact, shiny red, and it ran like a champ. Her brother, Asher, was drying the hood when the girls bounded out of the house. His short, wavy raven hair was gleaming wet with the warm day and the effort he had put in washing the car. Bree watched his muscles spring and flex around his loose tank top, his bronze skin browning further in the late spring sunshine.

Lord, he was a hunk. Too bad he was Nonnie's big brother—off-limits as far as she was concerned.

"That'll teach you to bet me, big brother."

"I can't believe you bet Nonnie that she couldn't eat a whole boysenberry pie," Bree jabbed Asher in the ribs.

"She's been known to put away an entire tray of chocolate macadamia nut cookies, you know. Anybody that could eat so much rich stuff could eat a pie too, Doofus."

Asher gave Bree a playful swat. She was such a mouthy pipsqueak—kind of like his sister.

"You need to get your facts straight, Bree. I bet her that she couldn't eat a whole boysenberry pie *a la mode*. There's a difference. What I still don't get is how it is physically possible to fit that much food into that 5 foot nothing, 90 pound body."

"You're just a sore loser," Nonnie teased.

Asher grabbed his sister around the neck and knuckled the top of her head as if to rub the hair off. She gave him a fake punch to the gut, though it didn't come close to harming his six-foot, broad, muscled frame.

Then he became serious. "I did more than wash the car, little sis. I checked all of the fluids and the tire pressures. Dad changed the oil the last time we were over at his place. You two be careful, okay? Look out for hosers. They'll try to run you off the road."

"I will. Thanks, Asher." Nonnie gave him a quick squeeze and hopped in the driver's seat. Bree threw her bag in the back and took her position as navigator. They were on their way!

"You're so lucky having a big brother, Nonnie."

"You always say that, Bree. If only you knew what a great big pain in the neck he can be, sometimes!"

"I know. I mean, I practically live at your house when you're not at mine, but you know what I mean. Sometimes

6

it would just be nice to have someone besides my mom looking out for me. You've got your dad and your brother. They would never let anything bad happen to you. You're just lucky, Non, that's all."

"Yep, I'm lucky. You do need to remember, though, that even though it's just you and your mom, she is just about the coolest mom you could ask for."

"That's true, too. We both have awesome moms. I'm gonna really miss them."

Both girls grew quiet. It didn't take much to make them pensive these days.

Highway 97 meandered South paralleling the Columbia River. They watched the sagebrush and rock-dotted mountains blur by as Nonnie expertly maneuvered past Wells Dam and the turn-off to Lake Chelan. They were just past the tiny town of Orondo, just fifteen miles from their destination when an enormous white-tailed deer leaped as if on springs out of an apple orchard directly into their lane.

Bree's last coherent thought amid the squealing brakes and the smell of burning rubber and fear was that the statuesque doe had lovely brown eyes and that it was so sad that they were all about to die.

CHAPTER TWO

The combination of surprise and lack of experience proved too much for Nonnie. She simply lost control of the car. They did clip the deer, but witnesses watched her bounce up and run away. The girls didn't fare so well.

After slamming on the brakes, Nonnie steered the car toward the shoulder where it hit the roadside gravel and spun. They continued to spin into the orchard where a huge old apple tree finally stopped them. They were wearing their seatbelts, but the car was too old to have airbags.

Nonnie's head hit the windshield and her ribcage and abdomen took the force of the immobile steering wheel. Her side of the car at least stayed intact.

The passenger side, however, took most of the force of the tree trunk, crumpling the dash and footboard directly into BreeAnn's lap. Both girls were knocked unconscious by the crash.

Bree came to first, tasting the grit that had flown through the open window, and feeling as though her left leg was being chewed up, the foot feeling strangely detached from all of the sensation. She first screamed in pain and then became frantic as she realized that her very best friend was passed out, facing her direction, her normally brown face looking very pale and very bloody.

"Nonnie! Non! Wake up!" Bree realized that her arms were free so she used them to cradle Nonnie's face. She knew from her first aid class that she needed to make sure to keep Nonnie's neck still. Then she yelled for all she was worth for someone to help them. Thank God it was broad daylight.

Help wasn't far. Several orchard workers had been spraying in the trees across the highway from the accident. There had also been two other motorists nearby. All of them converged at once on the car and the ambulance wasn't far behind.

Before Bree knew it, they were both being carefully extracted from the car and loaded into the ambulance. The scene was a blur of relief that they were being helped, and excruciating pain from her injuries. She was trying hard to listen to the EMT's and follow instructions, but she found herself incredibly distracted.

Nonnie was still and pale as a corpse on the stretcher next to hers. The EMT's worked steadily and calmly, starting IV's, monitoring vital signs, and finally, to Bree's horror, sticking a tube down her throat so that they could help her breathing.

It seemed like the longest fifteen miles of her life as they were rushed to the hospital in Wenatchee. She just kept repeating over and over, "God, please help Nonnie. Please help Nonnie. Help Nonnie. Nonnie. God, please."

The paramedic finally sedated Bree because her own injuries were serious enough to send her into shock. They were just pulling into the emergency entrance at Central Washington Hospital when Bree slipped back into the comforting arms of unconsciousness.

Bree awoke four hours later to her mother's muffled sobs. Lilly was sitting in the corner of Bree's tiny ICU room trying to smother the grief and fear that were gripping her heart as her little girl lay unconscious, but stable, and Penny's daughter and her doctors fought for Nonnie's life in a cold operating room.

"Mommy?"

Lilly's sob caught in her throat. BreeAnn hadn't called her "Mommy" in years. She rushed to Bree's side, saying a quick thank you to the heavens that her eyes were open again.

"What happened, Mom?"

"You and Nonnie were in an accident."

Bree's memory was jogged at the mention of her friend. She immediately tried to sit up, sending a shot of lightning white pain through her left leg. She paled as her mother gripped her hand tighter.

"Don't try to move, Chickadee. You've got a broken leg and lots of bruises. Just lie still, okay?"

"Nonnie." Bree's eyes filled with tears as she remembered Nonnie's condition when she'd last seen her.

She asked in a voice so small that Lilly had to strain to hear her, "Is she dead, Mommy?"

Tears spilled down Lilly's cheeks unchecked. "No, baby, she's not dead. But she's hurt real bad, Bree. They're in the operating room right now trying to patch her up."

"Where's Penny?"

"She and Asher are in the surgery waiting room. Nonnie's dad is on his way too. She's been in there for a few hours."

"What's wrong with her?"

"She hit her head pretty good on the windshield, but her brain seems to be okay. It's her belly that's not. She's bleeding internally and they went into surgery to see if they

10

can stop it."

Bree started crying fresh tears.

"Is she going to be okay?"

"We don't know, Chickadee. We just have to pray that she will be."

Bree felt suddenly exhausted, sad and worried beyond comprehension.

Lilly recognized it right away. "You need to rest, Bree. You've got some healing to do yourself. I'll just be right here when you wake up.

"No, Mom. Please. I know that I need to rest, but I want you to go be with Penny and Asher. They need you more than I do. I love you, and I'm awfully tired…."

"Shh. Sleep, Bree. I'll have your nurse come get me as soon as you're awake again."

Lilly slipped out of the room as soon as Bree drifted off to sleep a moment later.

⸺⸺

Lilly joined Penny and Asher just in time to see the surgeon enter the waiting room. Her body flooded with relief as she saw the obvious encouragement on his face.

Penny saw it too. She had stood up when she saw the doctor and she now sank back into her chair in a heap. "Thank God," she breathed as she made the sign of the cross on her chest.

"Mrs. Pakootas?"

"Yes."

"I didn't get the chance to meet you before we rushed your daughter into surgery. I'm Dr. Whitmore. I'll just cut to the chase, if you don't mind. Your daughter is a very lucky young woman. The impact she had with the steering wheel basically cut her liver in half. The lucky thing is that she received help quickly and that we had blood on hand to give her. We've repaired the liver laceration and she is stable. We still have a machine breathing for her until her body has time to recover from the immediate insult, but I expect if she does as well as she appears to be doing, that we will take the tube out by tomorrow.

"We will keep her in Intensive Care until that time, but I do believe that Nonnie is out of the woods. You can see her as soon as we move her from recovery to her room.

"I'm sure that you will have questions for me later, but I'll give you time to absorb the news first. I'll see you during my rounds this evening."

"Thank you so much, Dr. Whitmore. I am so grateful, to you and to God. I couldn't imagine life without my beautiful little Nonnie."

"She's a strong girl, Mrs. Pakootas. You're very welcome, but she did most of the work."

As he walked away, Asher enveloped Penny and Lilly in a bear hug and they sat to wait until they could see Nonnie. It was the first opportunity for Penny and Lilly to talk since their interminable ride from Pateros to Wenatchee.

"How's BreeAnn, then, Lilly?" Penny inquired.

"She's going to be okay, too. She broke her lower left leg pretty badly, both bones. But they were able to set it without surgery. Other than that, she just has some bruises. She's terribly worried about Nonnie. You know them. They've been inseparable for fifteen years. She was sure that she'd lost her best friend. She's getting some sleep now. I'll go tell her about Nonnie as soon as the nurse comes to get me."

"What would I have done, Lilly? I almost lost my little girl. I knew that she'd be going out on her own soon, but that was different. I never imagined that I could lose her entirely.

"Asher and Nonnie, they're my world. When their lousy dad left for that blond floozy, they acted like the grown-ups, cooking for me, doing the laundry and housework. My kids are extra special, but your babies are like that in general, aren't they?

She continued, "It's like, when you have this tiny, perfect baby, you realize that your whole life, your whole focus suddenly rests on another human being. You know what I mean, Lilly. You're a mother too."

Penny was going to continue babbling, but Lilly suddenly couldn't listen any longer. Because she didn't know, not exactly, and she knew that she could never tell her friend why.

CHAPTER THREE

It had always been like this between them. Penny, for
the life of her, couldn't figure it out. Whenever they started
talking about babies at the bakery or if Penny brought
babies up, Lilly would up and leave the conversation.

Like now, for instance, they just found out that her
baby was going to live and though she would admit that
she was rambling on a bit, Penny couldn't understand why
Lilly was suddenly making an excuse to go to the cafeteria
to get coffee. They had just decided a minute ago to sit and
wait for Nonnie to get to her room.

What did she say that made Lilly so uncomfortable?

Lilly was gone before she even had time to
contemplate. Her ex-husband was rushing through the door
as Lilly rushed out, giving her friend a reprieve as Penny
turned her furious attention to a man who hadn't made it
to the hospital until *after* his daughter was already out of
surgery. Nonnie could have died on the operating table and
Edward Pakootas wouldn't have even been on the premises.

"Where's Hannah? Did you have to drop your hussy
off at the nail salon before you came to see your own
injured daughter?"

She was really going to let him have it this time. It was
a good thing Asher was there to buffer the situation or she
would have gotten herself kicked out of the hospital for
poor conduct.

"I just got off work, Penny. I had to deliver a van to

Jeter's before closing. They're my biggest customer. I had to stay and finish the job or lose them for good. Forget Hannah for a minute, Penny. How's Nonnie?" He pleaded. He looked just as worried and frightened as Penny had been a few moments ago before talking to the surgeon. Penny softened a little.

"She's gonna make it, Ed." She saw a nurse signaling toward them as if to get their attention. "Let's go see our girl." Penny hooked her arm through Asher's and followed the nurse to the ICU with Edward in tow.

There were so many tubes and wires and machines that Nonnie was scarcely visible beneath them. The nurse had warned them that she was still very fragile. The largest danger, bleeding to death, had been removed, but Nonnie had now to overcome the risk of infection and the weakness that followed blood loss.

They would be allowed to see Nonnie and talk to her, squeeze her hand, but their visit would be limited to fifteen minutes and then they would be required to return to the waiting room. There were only two people allowed in the room, so Asher waited outside while his parents checked on their daughter.

Nonnie was still heavily sedated so that she wouldn't fight the tube down her throat. Penny cried softly and knelt to kiss her daughter's warm hand. Edward hung back at first and then brought a chair from the corner for Penny to sit in.

There were no rules, no recipes to follow as their emotions assaulted them. Edward, at a loss as to what to do next, walked behind his estranged wife, laying his hands lightly on her shoulders. They remained connected that way—Nonnie to Penny, Penny to Edward—until the nurse quietly notified them that they needed to wait outside.

Asher watched the whole scene unfold through the glass door to Nonnie's room. If only she could wake up and see this! He had never really believed that his dad had stopped loving his mom. Hannah was the kind of girl that a guy clung to only for a short time because her emotional depth was nil, her looks far outselling her personality. Edward had been beguiled, but at a huge cost to his family. Asher had sensed his regret pretty regularly over the last year.

Nonnie would bust her dad's chops if she was awake, for not laying a sloppy kiss on her himself, but Asher could understand why he was intimidated. When it came to his turn to visit, he chickened out, opting instead to return to the ICU waiting room with his tearful parents. They walked by BreeAnn's room on the way and Asher paused while his parents kept walking. He bid Bree a silent hello, watching her sleep for a moment.

If she hadn't been sleeping so peacefully, he would have stopped to tell her that Nonnie was improving. She would be terribly worried. The two of them were more like sisters than girlfriends. He honestly couldn't imagine one without the other. Asher shuddered as he thought of how close that had been to reality.

Lilly fled to the cafeteria. Between the trauma of finding out the girls had been in an accident and the relief of knowing that Nonnie would be okay, she had been *this close* to telling Penny everything.

How many times over the last ten years had Lilly been about to spill her secrets to Penny? The two of them talked constantly. It made the time pass while they baked and peddled their creations. She knew everything about Penny, from the note she passed to Edward in the fifth grade to see if he liked her, to the agony of the pending divorce.

And Penny knew everything about her, almost. Her history abruptly stopped at the moment she arrived in Pateros and opened her small bakery, armed with her grandmother's recipes and barely enough money to make the first month's rent. The area was so badly in need of a quality bakery that business took off immediately. It exploded the minute that Lilly hired Penny.

The girls had been friends right away. Lilly and BreeAnn had moved into a nineteen-foot trailer about the length of a pick-up truck away from the Pakootas' doublewide in the Double W Trailer Park. Two-year-old Bree had toddled right up to Nonnie and, after reverently stroking each of her silky, black braids, had grinned so big it nearly turned her face inside out. She then promptly stripped herself of her diaper, showing Nonnie how. Then both girls had run, shrieking and naked through the sprinkler watering the tiny, brown lawn.

They were neighbors for roughly a year. Lilly had by then scrimped enough to make rent on a decent two-bedroom house near the school. Geography didn't matter, though. By the time they were five, Bree and Nonnie rarely even spent a night apart. Baking meant very early mornings for Lilly, so it was a relief to her that Penny allowed Bree to stay over as much as she did.

When her finances allowed her to hire another baker, Lilly knew Penny, who had worked for years at the grocery store bakery six miles up the highway, would be the perfect choice. By then the kids were old enough to get themselves ready for school with a little help from Ed. Penny had jumped at the chance and over the years, they had become very good friends.

Penny never stopped trying to unlock Lilly's past, though, and there was so much that Lilly would never be able to tell her. It wasn't that she didn't trust Penny. She did. She just couldn't take a chance that BreeAnn would ever find out the truth. It would devastate both of their lives.

Bree awoke in a panic two hours later. 'Nonnie!' Her mom hadn't come back to tell her about Nonnie.

The room came into focus through the haze of painkillers. She still felt a dull ache in her leg, but it wasn't as sharp as it had been earlier. She could see that she was alone. Where was that button that was supposed to be on your bed to buzz the nurse?

She was digging around her bed when her mom came in looking drained. She was glad to see her mom, but alarmed to see her looking so glum.

"How's Nonnie, Mom?" Her first concern was that her friend was okay.

"She's gonna make it, Bree. She was injured really badly and she's still breathing through a tube, but the doctors are encouraged. They're watching her closely for infection, but she's stable. She's just a few doors away from here, actually."

"Have you gone to see her? Can I see her?"

"I have. She looks scary right now underneath all those

machines, but her coloring is okay. They're drugging her to keep her asleep until tomorrow so that she won't fight the tube.

"I would say that you could go see her, but you need to rest too, Bree.

"I've *been* resting. I want to see her, Mom," Bree whined. She was wretched with the thought of Nonnie not breathing on her own. Maybe she could will her well again if she just laid eyes on her. Oh, this day was supposed to have been so different. If not for that stupid deer, they would still be shopping!

"I'll see if you can be moved to a wheelchair, yet. The nurses here are awfully busy, especially looking after Nonnie. They said that they'll be moving you to the regular nursing floor in the next few hours since you're doing okay. Let's see if you can drop in on Nonnie on the way, okay?"

"I guess. I'm just glad she's going to be okay. I'll feel better if I see her, that's all."

It was almost ten o'clock by the time they came to take her to the second floor. She saw Nonnie, but it didn't make her feel any better. Nonnie looked like nothing more than a Raggedy Ann doll with a turban, tubes sticking out of every place from her mouth to her arms, to her legs, which had blue wraps around them.

The nurse explained all of it to her, trying to demystify her friend's plight just a little. The tube in her throat was for breathing. The tubes in her arms were for IV's and blood products. The tubes going to her legs were hooked to the blue plastic wraps, which would contract every few minutes to keep the blood moving back to her heart. The wires across her chest were there to help them monitor her heart rate. The thrumming, imposing machine in the corner was hooked to the tube down her throat, breathing for her when they told it to.

Bree just wanted to turn back time to that morning. Could that have been just twelve hours ago? She sighed, fat tears rolling down her cheeks. Her mom, who was pushing Bree's IV pole, gestured to the nurse that it was time to move on to Bree's new room.

These girls both had a lot of healing to do, physically and emotionally. More than ever, Penny and Lilly had their work cut out for them. Lilly secretly hoped she was worthy of the task.

CHAPTER FOUR

It was a week later and Bree was home, though she still hobbled about on crutches. Graduation was just a week away and she wasn't ready!

Nonnie was still a little weak, but recovering quickly. The doctors were giving her permission to go through the graduation ceremony, though she would have to be pushed in a wheelchair. Bree wanted to be the honorary pusher, but her crutches made this impossible. Someone else would have to be appointed.

If she thought she had a lot to do to prepare for the ceremony before, she certainly had a lot to do now. She still had to finish her speech. She also still needed to get dresses and accessories for both of them now that their shopping plans had been foiled. She planned to do that after visiting Nonnie on Sunday with her mom.

On top of that, she needed to gather baby pictures and senior pictures of both of them. One of the neighboring high schools had a tradition of doing a slide show with now and then photos of the seniors. A classmate had learned of the idea and, at the last minute, decided that he wanted to put together a show for their class. He needed two baby pictures and one senior picture and then he was going to scan them into his laptop to play on the overhead projector.

The pictures had been due at the school on Wednesday and of course everyone had been cool about hers and Nonnie's being late. But now it was crunch time and Tyler really needed the pictures to finish his show.

Penny had Asher dig out some pictures. One featured a very chubby Nonnie at six months and two others were of Nonnie and Bree together, grinning, their arms locked around each other's waist. They were clothed, which was unusual in those early years. Asher said he had to pass up several shots of them in their birthday suits. Bree wasn't sure, but she thought he reddened a little talking about them as naked babies.

The senior picture that he gave her was Bree's favorite. It was Nonnie on the dock at the Pateros waterfront. Her hair was glistening black and braided just as it had been the first time Bree had seen her. She was wearing a yellow tank top and a long tie-dyed sarong and she was leaning back on her arms, her smile mischievious and brilliantly white, her dark skin exotic and lovely.

She longed to see Nonnie this carefree again. Time would see to it, she hoped.

The next task should have been an easy one. She needed to get a baby picture of herself. She realized as she was heading home, though, that she had no idea where to look. Her mom wasn't much of a picture-taker. Penny had always been the one trying to catch the Kodak moments. Most of Bree's friends' homes were decorated with family pictures everywhere. Her mom had decorated instead with watercolors and sculptures.

Bree had asked her once why they didn't have any pictures of their family. Was it really just her and her mom always? Her mom had explained that she had liked photographs at one time in her life, and then fate had taken Bree's dad and her brother away from them. They had died in a terrible boating accident while out fishing together. Her mom had been vague on the details, but Bree guessed from conversations that their boat had been struck by a larger vessel and they both had drowned when it sank. Bree had been just a baby and she and her mom had been at home when it all happened.

Lilly and Bree's dad had both lost their parents when they were teenagers. Therefore, Bree had no grandparents either. Bree understood. Lilly didn't keep pictures up because they reminded her of all that she had lost. It was too painful to see their faces everyday.

Bree had comprehended the loss very well because though she couldn't remember them, in her heart she missed her brother and her dad desperately. She didn't bring the subject up to her mom for fear of hurting her more.

Now, though, she really needed to dive into her past again because she was expected to cough up a baby picture of herself.

When she got back to her house, it was quiet. Her mom was trying to catch things up at the bakery since they would be going back to Wenatchee the next day. Bree hobbled her way down the hallway to her mother's room. She hesitated at the door.

Her mom had always been very clear that her bedroom was off-limits to Bree and Nonnie. She called it her 'inner sanctum,' the one place where she could get away from everyone and have peace. Bree had been very respectful of that, even when Nonnie admitted that she had snooped in her parents' room before her dad left, just to see what they had in there. Bree couldn't even imagine 'snooping' through her mom's stuff!

That wasn't what she was doing. Her mom wasn't

home so she could ask about the pictures, so she was just going to look in a few places.

She remembered the time when she was thirteen that she had heard her mom sobbing in her room and she had gone to investigate. When she had knocked on the door, she had heard her mom wrestle the covers before she told Bree to come in. She had sat on the bed with her mom, stroking her hair as she cried and she had noticed the calico fabric on the hatbox that her mom had tried to shove under the comforter.

Being the dutiful daughter, she hadn't asked about it. All she needed to do now was find the hatbox. She was certain she would find there the pictures and the faces that she was looking for.

Bree started under the bed, laying herself and her crutches down. Her mom was very organized, she realized. Underneath the bed were Rubbermaid containers, labeled "Sweaters," "Spare Socks," and "Heavy Pajamas." Her collapsible rowing machine was under the other side of the bed. No hatbox there.

She tried the armoire next. No hatbox in the armoire. Okay, that left her mom's walk-in closet. There were lots of hatboxes in there. In fact, the top shelf was lined with them. She hadn't realized that her mom liked hatboxes so much. She had at least a dozen of them. Bree was going to be very frustrated if all they had inside them were hats!

There was no stopping now, so Bree took down the four boxes that had calico fabric on them, checking each one as she got it down. Two of them did have hats in them. Funny, she had never seen her mom wear a hat. Perhaps they had belonged to Lilly's mother. The other two hatboxes appeared to have a mix of photos and newspaper

24

clippings in them. She decided to start with those.

She scooted the hatboxes one at a time with her casted foot over to her mom's bed. She sat on the bed, taking a deep breath for fortification before delving into her own past, something that had been heretofore forbidden. She opened the first of the boxes to find an 8x10 glossy black and white photograph of her mother posing properly with another young woman very close to her age. 'Why, they look like sisters!' Bree thought. Her interest was piqued. Her mom had never mentioned a sister.

There were clippings of both Lillian and Shannon, whose name Bree obtained from the myriad of clippings. Their last name was Waters, another fact that Bree had not known about her mother, her maiden name. There were pictures of the two of them together at various ages and of their parents. So these people were her grandparents. The dad and his daughters had the same shade of gray for hair, making Bree assume that they all had honey-colored hair like Lilly. And her saucer-shaped, startling, violet-blue eyes could have only come from her mother. Her sister's eyes appeared darker, but the same unusual shape.

Bree looked like none of them. She looked up into the dresser mirror across the room and peered closer at her own white-blond shock of hair. Nonnie called it her 'feathers' because of the way her hair fluffed and frizzed and took flight in a slight breeze. She also assessed her eyes, the color of dried seaweed, and wondered why she looked nothing like her mother or her family.

She looked again. Okay, well, maybe she did have her mother's slightly upturned nose and her high, proud forehead, but that was about it. She'd always wondered if she looked like one of her grandparents. If she did, it must have been on her dad's side. Come to think of it, her mom did say once that she looked a lot like her dad and her brother.

She was all the way through the first box, so she put everything back carefully the way she had found it. There was no sense having her mother know what she'd been up to. Lilly would simply freak if she could see Bree now.

In the second hatbox, Bree finally found some baby pictures, though most of them appeared to have been taken after she was two and many included chubby baby Nonnie. Penny must have given Lilly copies. Bree was about halfway into the box when she noticed a postcard-sized piece of paper sticking out from the bottom of the pile of pictures. She grabbed it.

It was a little thinner than card stock. She recognized the format. It was one of those missing persons fliers like you would find on occasion in your mailbox. She had been throwing those away with the rest of the junk mail ever since her mom had started having her pick it up. When she turned this one over, though, she might have turned her whole world over as well.

Staring up at her was her mother's face, shiny and young and black and white, like it had just been in the photographs from the other hatbox. She quickly examined the other face to see which child had been missing in association with her mother. The baby pictured there was only about a year old, with giant, dark eyes and the most uncannily bald head she'd ever seen on a baby.

Bree still wasn't sure who it was and then she glanced over at the hatbox again. There in the pile of unexamined photos was a picture of Bree herself at two. She had more hair than the baby in the missing person photo, but it was undeniably BreeAnn who was pictured there next to her mother.

She read the caption: "Beatrice Devon. Missing since October 10, 1987. Date of birth March 15, 1986. Last seen at Cody Park, North Platte, NE. Last seen with Lillian Waters, pictured above. If you have any information about the above missing child……."

Someone was looking for her. What did this mean? Was she *kidnapped* when she was just a baby? And why would her mom take her? Who was she really? Her name was really Beatrice. At least her birthday wasn't a lie. How many other lies had she been told?

Her head swirled and she had to lie down. It seemed like hours later that she realized that she needed to collect herself. Nonnie, her source of common sense, wasn't here right now, so she would have to be sensible about this on her own. She gathered all of the materials from the second box and put them back the best she could. Except for the missing persons flier. While she replaced the hatboxes just the way she'd found them, she made sure that she kept that out.

Bree was going to get some answers, whether her mom liked it or not.

CHAPTER FIVE

Graduation went beautifully. Lilly felt bad about it, but she hadn't coughed up a baby picture for Bree (for good reason) and a picture of her and Nonnie had been altered instead to picture only Bree. Nobody had known the difference, except perhaps Bree herself.

Bree's speech was poignant as she talked about the influence teachers and her fellow graduates had on her formative years. She finished the speech in a manner that Lilly found sort of odd, saying, "Though I don't know myself as well as I once thought I did, I plan to make the most of this new opportunity for discovery and I challenge all of my classmates to do the same."

Maybe she was making reference to how the accident had changed her and her view of herself. All Lilly knew was that her normally very self-possessed daughter all of a sudden seemed withdrawn and quiet and unsure of herself.

How could she possibly expect her to be unaffected by the accident, though? Bree's best friend had nearly died and she herself had a cast and crutches and the continual need for painkillers, though she was weaning herself off of them gradually as she healed.

It was just that BreeAnn had never *avoided* her the way she seemed to lately. It was unsettling. When Lilly mentioned Bree's attitude to Penny, she chalked it up to an eighteen-year-old cutting the purse strings. If a teenager didn't act that way, she reasoned that you would never want him or her to leave. Asher had been an incredible pain in the rear his final year of high school, but by the time he'd finished his associate's degree two years later, Penny was glad to have him home again.

Penny could be of little help anyway. Other than providing advice and moral support over baked bread, she didn't have time to deal with Lilly's misgivings. Nonnie was home now and, unexpectedly, so was Edward. He had come to his senses regarding his family and moved back in. Penny made light of the new living situation, but she lit up like a young girl every time she talked about it. She still categorized Ed as a louse, but she was giving him credit for trying to make up for it.

Nonnie was well on her way to recovery. Her wound was healing and she still had to take it easy. Her banged up forehead had healed some, but she still had a scab in the center. Bree teased her that she looked like Charles Manson when she smiled, only with a star instead of a swastika. Nonnie simply responded with Bree's new nickname— "Hop-Along White."

The girls were inseparable once again. Perhaps that was why Lilly felt neglected. She hardly saw Bree anymore because she was always with Nonnie, taking care of her, she said. It was bad enough that she was going off to college in the fall; Lilly was losing Bree already.

***

Bree and Nonnie were doing far more than healing together. They were researching and planning. Nonnie's first reaction to Bree's revelation about her past was to suggest marching Bree right down to the Brewster Police Department and handing her over to them. After all, she'd been missing for over sixteen years. *Somebody* had to still be looking for her.

Bree admitted it would be the simple solution to just tell the cops who she really was and let them do the rest. It would also be easy to log onto the Internet and turn herself in to the Center for Missing and Exploited Children, the people who had put together the flier. She'd checked. All it would take was a phone call or a click of a mouse to be found again.

There was just one thing stopping her—Lilly. Bree was angry with her. She just couldn't believe that her own mom had kept such a huge secret from her all of these years. She'd always thought they were close, closer than almost any mom and her daughter. Sharing everything—them against the world. Lilly never limited her, yelled at her, belittled her. She was quietly supportive, encouraging, and trusting of her daughter.

But she hadn't been honest, had she? Not even close. Knowing what she did know about their relationship, though, Bree couldn't take any step that might get her mother in trouble. The thought kept niggling that her mom must have had a darn good reason to take her away, change their names, and hide her all these years.

So Bree and Nonnie were doing their research on the World Wide Web, collecting information on little Beatrice Devon. She accessed the archives from the North Platte Bulletin around the date of her disappearance, requesting the materials with Nonnie's address and the promise of a C.O.D.

Nonnie and Bree pored over two weeks worth of papers and finally found brief mention of a local citizen reporting the sighting of Beatrice and Lilly at Cody

Park. It had been widely televised that the girl had been missing for a month from her home in St. Louis. Her father, a prominent psychiatrist, had offered a reward for information leading to her recovery. The article listed the missing persons phone number.

Bree went immediately online to access the yellow pages for St. Louis, Missouri. There couldn't be that many Dr. Devons practicing psychiatry there. Indeed, there were two: Milton Devon, Sr. and Milton Devon, Jr.

Bree had no idea how old her brother would be now, but she figured he couldn't possibly be old enough to be graduated from medical school. So she deduced logically that Dr. Milton Devon, Jr. would be Beatrice's, her, dad.

It took them all of two weeks to have Dr. Devon's business and personal address and phone number. They even found him on Classmates.com and figured him to be fifty-two by his graduation date.

It was a scorching early July day and Nonnie and Bree sat back on Nonnie's bed, satisfied that they had all of the information they needed.

"Now what?" Bree asked.

"Now you know who you really are, Bree. Or should I call you Bea?"

"Don't confuse me, Non. It has seemed so unreal while we've been searching. It's been like detective work. Only I don't relate to Beatrice Devon at all. I'm having trouble wrapping my mind around the fact that she's me."

"That's understandable. I'm having trouble doing the same."

"So what do I do now? Just show up on my dad's doorstep and say, 'Hey, I'm your long lost, kidnapped daughter?'"

"What else is there to do? I guess you could write him a letter and see what he does."

"Mom could get in trouble if I do that because he'd be able to trace it back to Pateros."

"We could pay for a trial membership at Classmates. com and get his email address. That would be a little harder to trace."

"But not impossible. No, Nonnie, I can't risk that Mom will get caught. You know how upset I am with her, but I want to give her a chance to explain herself, if that's possible."

"Are you going to confront her now that you have the information you need?"

"I don't know. She's noticed that I'm avoiding her. I just don't know what to say anymore."

Nonnie couldn't offer any advice, so she just listened. She knew Bree wasn't spending much time at home because she was always with her. She didn't mind. After all, they'd always been more like sisters than friends anyway. Nonnie just wished she could keep Bree out of her Reese's Pieces. The doctor had just cleared her to eat whatever she wanted and she wasn't ready to share those yet!

In all seriousness, though, she couldn't imagine the emotions Bree was having, suddenly realizing her whole life was a lie.

"What if I didn't tell her, Nonnie? What if we just took a road trip?"

"You know they'll never let us do that after my attack on the mighty doe. Besides, I don't have a car anymore."

"I thought your dad was fixing one up at his shop for you."

"He is, but I'm not sure when it'll be ready." Bree could see the shadows in Nonnie's eyes when she talked of driving again. She wasn't just afraid of it. She was terrified.

Bree moved to her friend and gave her a quick, gentle squeeze. "Don't worry, Non. I won't make you drive me to St. Louis. Maybe we could just hop on a bus."

"From here? I guess we could hitchhike to Wenatchee and go from there."

"You two will hitchhike over my dead body."

Bree and Nonnie looked up in surprise to find Asher leaning against Nonnie's door jam. He looked imposing, arms crossed over his chest, frowning his disapproval of any road trip.

"Asher! We were just joking about hitchhiking. I was just telling Nonnie that I wouldn't make her drive again." Bree was nervous that he might have heard the rest of their conversation.

"It wasn't Nonnie's fault that the deer ran out in front of her, so she'll drive again someday if Dad and I have anything to say about it. But that's not what I'm worried about. I know you two are up to something. You've been plotting for weeks and it's time to spill." Asher was adamant.

"We don't have to tell you anything, big brother. This is a free country."

"You forget, smart girl, that I am sworn by Mom and Dad to make sure nothing else bad ever happens to you and that includes Bree. I know something's up and you know how stubborn I can be."

Bree didn't want any trouble from Asher and it was her secret to tell. What harm could there be in telling him their plans? She trusted Asher. He wouldn't tell Lilly if Bree asked him not to.

"I found out my mom kidnapped me when I was a baby," she blurted out. Asher's mouth fell open and he sunk to the couch across from Nonnie's bed.

Before she knew it, she was telling Asher the whole story. He was disconcerted and amazed and before the end of Bree's explanation, he was determined to help her get to St. Louis. It was the only way to find out more about Bree's past without hurting Lilly and it was obvious that no one wanted to do that.

What they needed was money—and a plan. That was where he came in.

CHAPTER SIX

Asher Pakootas had learned a few things in his short run as the man of the house. He had come home after finishing his first two years of school, thinking that he would start back at a four-year school in the fall. He wanted to be an elementary school teacher.

That had been over a year ago. He hadn't returned to school because his Mom and his sister had needed him after Edward left. Penny was terrible with money and Asher immediately began to oversee the finances. Nonnie was crushed by her parents' separation and she simply needed her big brother for support and encouragement.

So Asher had put his education plans on hold and taken a job working nights at the local convenience store. He was saving everything he could so that his final two years would be paid for. He was bored, but his mom and Nonnie were worth every moment of boredom.

Now that Edward had gotten his act together, Asher was looking more seriously at the possibility of leaving for Eastern Washington University in the fall. He knew he could always return to his hometown later, but he wanted to come back with skills to offer.

Until he had walked in on Bree and Nonnie's conversation earlier, September had been the month of mass exodus for all of them. That hadn't changed even with the accident. This discovery of Bree's, though, was huge. How could they all go their separate ways and not help her reconcile with her confusing past?

He and Nonnie were going to have to help her. The way Asher saw it, they had the rest of July to get their plans made and the month of August to execute them. He was going to spend evenings at his dad's shop getting Nonnie's new car finished. After all, his only wheels were a motorcycle and he couldn't possibly fit all three of them on that.

Since he was the financial whiz of the group, he would be making their budget. He had plenty of money stashed away and he offered it to Bree, but she refused to take his college money. She had been saving her babysitting and lawn-mowing money for as long as she could remember. Her mom gave her an allowance, so she had just never needed to spend any of it. Bree had about three hundred dollars saved.

Asher figured that they would eat through that by the time they hit the Nebraska State line. They could save money by camping along the way and he had mapped out every KOA from Idaho to Missouri. But they still needed money for campground fees, gas, food, and any emergencies. None of them had a credit card, so he was going to apply for one just in case.

Nonnie was still recovering, so Bree and Asher vetoed the idea of her getting a job for the month of July. They also knew that their moms would be entirely too suspicious if she and Bree became suddenly enterprising. They needed another five hundred dollars to be safe.

They had a whole month and Bree had a solution. She and Nonnie were going to pilfer it. Edward was forever leaving ones and fives lying around after he emptied his pockets each day. Penny left her purse in plain sight on the kitchen table every night. Nonnie was just going to take a few dollars here and there that her parents would never miss.

Lilly paid herself twice a month according to the bakery's success. Bree had watched her routinely cash out about a third of each of the checks and make a stash in the top drawer of her hall secretary. Whenever cash was needed for groceries or shopping trips, Lilly would break into the "Cash Stash." Bree was pretty sure that Lilly didn't keep close track of how much was in there at any given time. So she was going to raid it slowly over the course of the month, a twenty, a five, a few ones at a time.

Asher would make up the difference from his wages.

They made their plans, each anticipating in a different way: Bree was nervous, anxious to get it all over with; Nonnie was apprehensive about being on the highway, knowing how vulnerable she had been just a few short months before; Asher was just plain excited about getting out of town for while.

They would leave the first of August.

⊱──⊰

"Stop it, Edward!" Penny grinned at her tall, broad-shouldered husband and gave him a playful swat.

"What? I can't take a little pinch of that nice tush?" Edward teased Penny, happy to have her full attention.

"Not while I'm trying to roll out this pie crust. You're likely to get lambasted by my rolling pin!"

"Hey, no threats with deadly weapons on my watch," Lilly joined in, enjoying the fun banter. After all, she had seen Penny far too miserable over the last year. She needed to relish every moment of this reconciliation. They all did.

37

"Hey, Lilly, can I have one of those cream cheese cinnamon rolls, pretty please."

"Ed, have mercy. You know I can't resist when you point those sad brown eyes at me," Lilly put her hands over her eyes as if to ward off Edward's appeal.

"You wouldn't be the first woman to feel that way, Lilly," Penny said, and then immediately regretted her words, for the playful mood instantly fizzled at her comment. Edward reddened and looked down at his shoes.

"Aw, Ed, I'm sorry," she immediately tried to make up for the jibe. "You know I didn't mean it that way. You remember what the counselor said. I've got all that time being angry to forget about. I'm working on it. Honey, I really am."

"Shiny Penny. I know you're trying. We both are. I'll forgive you this time if you just put your lips right here." He pointed to his puckered lips.

Lilly busied herself boxing up a cinnamon roll for Ed while the two of them kissed and made up.

"How's Nonnie's car coming along? I've noticed you and Asher spending quite a lot of time at the shop," Lilly finally interrupted. Edward's shop was a block and a half away across the street from The Duck Hotel. Because her storefront faced the parking lots of many of the neighboring businesses, Lilly could see Edward Pakootas' shop from her front counter.

"Yeah, Asher's on the evening shift at the quick stop, so he's been spending the early mornings working on the car. I think it'll be okay for her. It's got more metal than the red one had because it's older and by the time we get done, it'll run great too."

Lilly could tell that Penny in particular didn't like the

idea of Nonnie driving again, but they all knew that the accident had been a freak thing. Their fear aside, it would be best for Nonnie if she did get behind the wheel again. After all, she had to be ready to drive to San Francisco in the fall and she needed her car there to get places for her training and to get to school from her cousin's house in Sonoma.

"I gotta get back, girls. Thanks for the breakfast. Don't work too hard." Ed gave the back of Penny's neck a quick squeeze with his work-roughened dark hands, winked, and smiled as he went out the door.

"What have the girls been up to these days, Penny? You know I never get to see my daughter anymore, except to say goodnight when she comes home to sleep."

Penny looked up from trimming piecrusts. Lilly had stopped mixing apple filling for the moment. Penny saw the concern there and she needed to be honest with her friend.

"I thought they were just hanging out, Lilly. You know, that Nonnie was feeling crummy and BreeAnn was over to keep her company and help her out and all of that. But Nonnie's been feeling better. She's bouncing around and eating like a horse and tormenting her brother just like the old days."

"I'm so glad to hear that, Penny. We all thought after the accident that she might never be the same again."

"Well she's not exactly the same. Her eyes get sort of haunted-looking when we bring up driving again and she really just won't talk about the accident at all. I don't think she really remembers much of it. I hope she's working past it.

"It's not really Nonnie who's got me worried, though, Lilly. It's Bree. She's avoiding me just like you said she's been avoiding you. She's never done that. You know that I've always felt like she was my other daughter. The girls and I used to sit and eat a whole pint of Haagen-Daas together and talk about everything from music to PMS. Bree hardly even looks my direction anymore when she's at the house.

"They spend all of their time in Nonnie's room searching the Internet and talking with the door closed. They don't even come out to watch movies anymore or play games in the kitchen. What's worse is that Asher, who has always been the pariah big brother as far as they were concerned, now seems to be their best friend. That does it for me, Lilly. They are up to something."

Lilly raised her eyebrows in alarm. She had always been jealous of Penny's ability to read their kids. That was why she was so worried now. If Penny thought the kids were up to something, then they needed to tread carefully, and to stop them before they did something stupid.

"We can't let them know that we're onto them, Penny. But you need to be my spy since they're at your house."

"Ed and I are on the case," Penny reassured her. "Besides they don't have too much more time to get in trouble. It's July twenty-fifth. They'll all be out of here in September. What kind of trouble could they possibly cause in that short period of time?"

CHAPTER SEVEN

The morning of August first felt like many Eastern Washington summer mornings: clear, cloudless, and dry. Asher had returned from his work shift at midnight and kept himself awake until three when his mom left for the bakery. Then, careful not to disturb his dad who was asleep in his parents' bedroom, he scratched his fingernails on Nonnie's door. She opened the door instantly. She had been waiting for him to make the signal.

She already had her duffel over her shoulder, as did Asher. Now all they needed was Bree. She was meeting them at the shop. Asher had Nonnie's keys to her new car in his pocket. It was parked out in front of the shop, ready to go (in the nick of time, too. He and Ed had finished tuning it up just the morning before.)

Bree was meeting them at the shop after her mom left for the bakery too. Nonnie and Asher were concerned when they got to the shop and she wasn't there yet. They sat in the cool morning air atop their duffel bags on the curb, silence reigning except for the occasional appeal of a cricket. Just when Asher was about to get annoyed at Bree, she popped silently into view, knapsack in tow.

"Sorry," she whispered. "The *owner* of the bakery was apparently running late this morning. Looks like her loyal employee was on time."

"We gotta be quiet, Bree. You can tell us in the car," Asher warned and opened the back door for both girls to

41

jump in with their bags. They could rearrange the trunk later after they were well out of town and after they'd picked up the rest of the stuff they needed for their trip.

He'd stashed tents and sleeping bags and canned food and camping supplies in a shed behind his friend Ian's house in Brewster. Ian, a high school social studies teacher, would have been suspicious of the stash had he not been hiking for the summer in Canada. Asher knew he never locked the shed and that he would never know what a nice storage place it had made for a few weeks.

Asher hopped into the driver's seat and started the car. He winced at the sound of the loud engine firing up. Chevy Impala's were pretty sweet old hotrods with big engines and his dad was right: There was more metal around them for sure. But the rumbling, cold engine cut through the still morning like a knife through butter. They needed to get out of here.

A block and a half away, Lilly was in a rush to catch up to Penny in their morning preparations. She hurried back to the refrigerators against the back walls and started to pull out trays heaped full of unbaked cookies. They needed to warm up just slightly before being popped into the oven. She looked up and out the storefront just in time to see brake lights come on at Ed's shop. That was odd, she thought. Usually the morning was still around their busy bakery.

"Penny, quick, do you see those brake lights over at the shop?"

"Yeah. Huh. Who do you suppose that is this time of morning?"

They continued to watch as the car backed out of the driveway and pulled onto the street.

42

"They don't have their headlights on."

"Well it *is* starting to get light out," Penny replied. Then she paused. "Hey wait a minute. That's Nonnie's new car. It's big and it's yellow. That's gotta be it. I didn't know they were done with it yet."

"You'd better call Edward and wake him up, Penny. We may have just seen your daughter's car get stolen."

Penny called Edward. His immediate decision was to get Asher up to help him check out the situation at the shop in case any thieves had been left behind.

But Asher wasn't there. His bed was empty and neatly made. That was odd. He knew Asher had come home from the convenience store because he had fallen asleep watching *Lethal Weapon* when Asher came in. Asher had given him a shake and told him to go to bed.

Maybe Nonnie would know where he had gone. By now it was four o'clock. It was awfully early to wake her, but she would understand when he told her the car was gone.

He knocked on her door. No response. He opened it and found Nonnie's room the mess that it normally was. Clothes were strewn on the floor hither and yon. Her vanity was littered with pots of creams and palettes of makeup. It looked like a pizza box was sticking out from under the mattress of her unmade bed. He would have to check that out later and make sure it wasn't going to stink. But there was no Nonnie either. Edward was perplexed and now he was also considerably more worried than he had been before. Where were his kids?

Then it occurred to him. What if they took the car?

He called Penny back and told her not to call the cops yet. She hung up the phone in frustration.

"Our kids are gone, Lilly. Edward thinks they may have taken the car."

"Why would they do that this time of morning? Where could they possibly be going?"

"Was Bree home when you left, Lilly?"

Lilly panicked. It hadn't occurred to her that Bree might be with Asher and Nonnie. What if they were all running away together?

"She was. I peeked in on her when I left and she was in her bed asleep."

"You'd better go home and check on her again. I'll take care of things here.

Lilly shed her apron and baking cap and bolted for the door. She drove the five minutes to her house and ran inside. She flung open Bree's door. She was gone. Her bed was made, though, and there was a neatly typed note in the middle of it.

Dear Mom—

You're going to be furious with me for being so sneaky, I know, but I want to say, first of all, don't worry. Nonnie and Asher and I have decided to take a road trip. We just all figured that this would be our last chance to do something fun together before we went our separate ways. We knew you would never let us go willingly after our accident, so we planned it behind your backs. I'm sorry and please tell Penny and Edward that we are sorry as well for making you all worry.

Aside from the way we left, please trust us on this. We are good kids. Remember? And we needed to do this. We

will call you from the road every couple of days to let you
know that we're okay. I love you, Mommy.
  BreeAnn

Lilly sat incredulously on Bree's daisy print comforter. Penny had said they were up to something, but this was so much bigger than she thought. Maybe they had wanted to avoid a fight, but she and Penny and Edward weren't totally unreasonable. They would have conceded eventually given the right argument. Now their kids were gone on a road trip.

They hadn't left an itinerary, a time frame, or any way to reach them. None of them had cell phones to her knowledge. Who knew how that old car was running?

Bree said not to worry. Well, that was impossible. She was going to worry plenty. For now, though, she needed to call Penny. She was probably getting frantic herself.

Edward was livid. He was frustrated with the girls for being so sneaky. He was furious with Asher for deceiving him about the car. He understood now why Asher had been so diligent, so dedicated to getting the work done. He had half a mind to call the police anyway and report the car stolen. That'd fix the punk for stealing Nonnie's car. Problem was, the eighteen-year-old, registered owner was in the car with him. They'd get a good scare, but none of them would actually get in trouble.

Each of them went on with their jobs that day. They met at Penny and Edward's house after work and drank iced tea and discussed their confounded children. They were going to let this slide so long as the kids did as promised and called them every couple of days. In the meantime they would have to trust them.

By nightfall on the first day, Asher had driven them as far as Billings, Montana. Loading up and leaving town had been surprisingly easy. Asher was organized. He was dog-tired, though, so after noon, Bree and even Nonnie took turns driving. The Impala was in great shape, comfortable and speedy through Montana, a state with no speed limit.

Asher was surprised at the ease with which they had left. He had half expected the police to issue an APB on them and to see flashing lights in his rearview at any moment.

Bree assured him that it was her letter that had made their escape possible. Her mom was big on the trust thing and she did trust Bree. It was too bad, as he reminded her, that she was such a liar. He got a bruise on his biceps muscle for that comment.

They settled into their campsite at the Billings KOA and ate canned chili that they heated up on their kerosene stove. Then they laughed the rest of the evening as they did as kids do and competed for the loudest emission resulting from their chili consumption. They stopped when the neighbors kindly, but firmly, explained their rudeness to them.

Asher finally gave in to sheer exhaustion. He figured that, with the exception of the catnaps in the car, he had been up for forty-two hours. He dove into his pup tent and fell asleep instantly.

Nonnie and Bree conceded to their tiredness a short time later and went to their dome tent. They talked softly for a little while in their sleeping bags. Bree was worried about what she would find out in St. Louis. Nonnie shared how grateful she was to Asher and Bree for getting her on the road again. Driving still made her nervous but she needed to do it. She really did feel safer in the great big Chevy. Nonnie and Bree drifted off to sleep feeling good about life and friendship and the beautiful state of Montana.

The balmy summer night bid them adieu, filling their dreams with mountain highways and untamed rivers and the laughter of close friends. If Bree sensed at all the twisted web that was going to entangle her in a few days, her dreams gave nothing away. She slept like a baby.

CHAPTER EIGHT

August 2nd was a Wednesday. The KOA in Billings should have been slow on a weekday, except that summer vacations were waning and families were out in mass trying to soak up the last juices of summer fun. Asher was apparently aloof to the rules of hygiene in a closed car—he refused to wait in line for the shower. Nonnie and Bree, on the other hand, wouldn't stand for staying grungy. They waited amongst preening teenagers and stuck-up college students to get a shower.

After what seemed like hours, Asher watched the girls emerge looking as if they'd done battle just getting cleaned and clothed. Their hair was still wet and they wore no makeup. Asher marveled, as he always did, at BreeAnn's white blond hair. Wet and slicked back, it looked the same shade as her pale skin. Her dramatic olive eyes stood out all the more without that floaty hair mussing about her face. Bree didn't think she was pretty, Asher knew. He disagreed. She was curved in the right places and she was natural. Her look was pleasantly unique.

As she smiled and playfully pinched him on the chest in greeting, he remembered what her gleaming, sweet-clean beauty had made him forget. She was a pipsqueak, just like his sister.

"What is wrong with these campgrounds that they can't provide a decent outlet for a hairdryer?" Nonnie exclaimed. "You should have seen it, Asher. All of these girls were turning over the nozzle of the hand dryer and blow-drying their hair! I watched one girl reach for her makeup bag under the dryer and almost knock herself out on it when she raised up."

"She was really hurt, so I tried really hard not to laugh. But it was pretty comical, almost too stupid to be real," Bree added.

Asher was unimpressed. "It took you guys forever," Asher complained. "I thought these people were on vacation. What are all of those girls doing in the bathroom at seven a.m.? We gotta hit the road."

"Well, apparently they have to leave too," Nonnie retorted. "I bet the line was a lot shorter at the men's. Since you're determined to build on your heinous body odor, did you at least get us some food for the road?"

"I figured I'd better since our schedule just got shot to heck. We have at least ten hours to get to North Platte, remember? All of the stuff is already packed. There are raspberry-filled doughnuts on the back seat and an orange juice for each of us. Let's hit the highway."

"Ugh. You call these doughnuts, Asher? They're in a box with a cellophane window. They were probably baked two years ago."

"Spoken like the daughter of a baker," Bree laughed. "Come on, Non. These are pretty good. Just don't inhale the powdered sugar on the outside. It makes you cough something fierce."

"Will you squirts get in the car already?" Asher shook his head. These women were going to drive him crazy.

They ate their breakfast quietly as they left the high

desert climate of Billings and traveled toward Hardin, Montana nearby the site of the infamous Battle of Little Bighorn, otherwise known as "Custer's Last Stand." Asher had always been a history buff and he would have loved to stop, but they had a whole day of driving ahead of them.

This wasn't really a road trip. It was a mission of discovery. Sightseeing would have to come some other time--maybe on the way home. They didn't really talk about that leg of the trip much. No one knew what Bree would find in St. Louis, or if she would even come back with them. She would be at a crossroads once she met her dad. She didn't know what she would want to do. She didn't like to talk about it much either. Just thinking about it gave her a headache.

They stopped for lunch in Buffalo, Wyoming at the foot of the Bighorn Mountains. Asher had read up on the town and learned that they could dine in a place that had once hosted Calamity Jane, Buffalo Bill Cody, Butch Cassidy and the Sundance Kid. The Occidental Hotel was home of The Virginian Restaurant. The food was excellent, though a little out of their budget, but they all enjoyed the slice of western history.

After such a crummy breakfast, Nonnie was particularly glad to get a decent meal.

They made their visit to Buffalo brief and switched freeways so that they could head South. They would traverse the entire North to South path through Eastern Wyoming before they cut across to North Platte, Nebraska.

They enjoyed the change in landscape from foothills and evergreens to the dry, high desert climate of Casper. They noticed as they approached southern Wyoming that trains were a prominent part of the landscape at all times of the day. Unlike the train that traveled through Pateros just twice a day, these train tracks were occupied constantly.

The hub of the railroad for Wyoming appeared to be the State capital, Cheyenne. As they approached the State capital, they saw the plains widening out to the East as far as the eye could see. It was breathtaking. They were from a valley surrounded by mountains. The vastness of the plains surrounding Cheyenne were almost overwhelming to them. It was so flat!

Because their lunch had been so long, they made a short dinner stop at a fast food restaurant near the freeway. Despite the beautiful and constantly changing landscape under the cloudless azure skies, the untold miles were wearing them out. Asher had driven until mid-afternoon when Bree had taken over so that he could get a nap. Nonnie took over after dinner for the straight drive on I-80 that would lead them to North Platte. Asher and Bree both piled into the back seat so they could nap more comfortably.

Bree woke Asher up as she tilted to the side and her head wound up on his shoulder. Her feathery white hair tickled his nose, so he put a hand on top of her head and let it rest there. Her hair was impossibly soft. She still smelled of lavender shampoo. He was just dozing off again and beginning to dream of Bree, when Nonnie slammed on the brakes.

She let out a guttural moan and then pulled off the freeway on the nearest exit. Bree and Asher, wide awake by now, gripped the front seat as Nonnie screeched to a stop.

"What in the world? Non, what's going on?" Bree shook off sleep as she climbed over the seat and slipped her arms around her friend. Nonnie was shaking.

"It was a deer, next to the freeway. Only it looked different. Its horns stuck straight up off its head instead of out to the side and it was a little smaller, but I just knew it was going to run out in front of me."

"Okay, Sis. That must've been really scary, huh? But you did good, Nonnie. You didn't hit it," Asher was still a bit shaken himself, but his main concern was the mental health of his sister. She'd never drive again if this kept up.

"And you didn't run off the road either, Non," Bree added.

"There wouldn't have been any trees to hit here anyway," Nonnie quipped, letting out a nervous giggle. She was going to be okay.

"You probably scared the daylights out of that antelope!" Bree laughed back.

"You think that's what it was?" Nonnie wasn't sure. She hadn't seen anything but a picture of an antelope before.

"Sounds like it, but I'm sure it's long gone by now. Wonder how much rubber you left on the road." Asher teased.

"I'll drive," he added as he came around to the driver's seat, letting Nonnie into the back. Bree stayed up front with him. "There's only a few hours left and then we can find a place to crash in North Platte. Will you break open the beef jerky and Pepsi, Bree?"

Asher continued down the exit and found the way to the entrance ramp about a half-mile away. Then they were on their way again to the place where little Beatrice Devon was last spotted sixteen years ago.

By the time they reached North Platte, they were utterly sick of looking at cornfields and trains. It felt like it had been days since they had left Billings. Bree's left leg was aching and her rear was asleep and Nonnie swore she was going to have to run a mile just to get her blood circulating again. They were tired and cranky.

Asher couldn't wait to be rid of them and their complaints if only for a short while. They got directions on the way into town for Cody Park. Luckily, there were campsites there as well. It was about 8 o'clock and it was starting to get dark. They had also seen clouds boiling up over the horizon as they approached town. Asher put the tents up as quickly as he could while Bree and Nonnie used the bathroom. They came back in time to help him finish unloading their bags into the tents.

The first strike of lightning was frighteningly near the park. Thunder rumbled around them, making the earth shake under their feet. Thunder and lightning storms were common to Eastern Washington, but those were most commonly accompanied by little or no rain. The deluge that followed that first lightning strike that night was unlike any they had ever seen. They couldn't even see the car fifteen feet away from their campsite.

They only had one tarp, so they abandoned Asher's pup tent completely, quickly taking his duffle and sleeping bag into the girls' tent. Asher ordered Nonnie into the tent, not wanting her to overdo, since she was still healing. Bree stayed to help Asher. Already soaked to the skin, they nonetheless stayed out in the storm long enough to tie the tarp down to the tent stakes.

Bree lost herself for a moment as Asher started stripping down to his underwear before he got in the dry tent. She'd never really gotten a look at his hairless, muscular brown body before, especially not sparkling wet as the flashes of lightning lit his body.

Asher caught her staring. With a flush of embarrassment and something else, attraction maybe, he grinned at Bree. "Your turn," he yelled above the downpour.

Bree caught the teasing challenge in his voice. She felt an unfamiliar tingle of excitement as she stripped down to her bra and panties.

Asher's breath caught. She was gorgeous. The raindrops made enticing rivulets down her face onto her chest between her full breasts, the nipples visible through her thin bra. Her smile flashed fluorescent in the stormy light. Her green eyes had begun to glow as well.

He became suddenly serious. This was unexplored and forbidden territory. His sister would kill him. He reached for Bree anyway.

Bree gasped as Asher pulled her close. She could feel his obvious attraction to her through their underwear. His skin was searing hot against her rain-drenched skin. He was going to kiss her! And she was going to let him.

"What *are* you two doing out there?" Nonnie yelled from inside the dome tent. "Are you *trying* to get struck by lightning?"

As if to punctuate her question, another streak of lightning flashed across the sky, fingers reaching simultaneously toward the plain. Asher and Bree broke apart guiltily, but reluctantly.

"Time to get inside, Bree."

"After you, Asher," Bree insisted, admiring his slim behind through his boxer briefs as he dove into the tent. By the time she got inside, he had stripped the briefs and thrown them out of his sleeping bag toward the entrance.

He politely turned his head as Bree did the same.

"Oh, great. I've got two naked companions tonight," Nonnie complained, totally oblivious to the electrical undercurrent that had nothing to do with the lightning.

"Let's hope there's no tornado with this lightning. I'm not making a run for it with you all in your birthday suits."

"Shut up, Squirt," Asher replied. He was back to his old bossy, big brother self. Thank goodness Nonnie had intervened. Because once he started with Bree, he didn't know how he would ever stop.

They stayed awake until they just couldn't any longer, the storm raging around them. Bree couldn't help but think that perhaps she wasn't welcome here. Mother Nature wasn't exactly smiling on the return of little Beatrice. She prayed that the morning would bring tranquility to Cody Park and some faint memory of who she was before her identity was stripped away for her. And she fell asleep for a while despite the earth-shaking thunder.

CHAPTER NINE

It had been two days and they still hadn't called. Lilly and Penny found themselves staring at the phone at every lull. The kids knew the phone number to the bakery by heart.

Lilly had trusted BreeAnn's note. Now she was feeling a little disconcerted about doing so. What had happened to the kids keeping in touch? She didn't know where in the world Bree was and that bothered her immensely. What if someone recognized her? That wasn't possible, was it, after all of these years?

Edward and Penny were also concerned. It was like Nonnie to do something spontaneous and not tell them about it. The accident had changed her, no doubt about it. She was more pensive, more philosophical, but she was still the same unpredictable, volatile girl, just with a touch of new vulnerability. This impromptu road trip was right up her alley.

But Asher, he was usually the responsible child. Ever the big brother, and for a while, the man of the house, Asher wasn't prone to flightiness like his sister. He mapped out everything ahead of time. He set goals. He budgeted his time and his money. He was also honest with them. Even when Edward was screwing up all of their lives and moving out, Asher pulled no punches. Edward never had any doubt where his son stood.

This trip and especially remaining incommunicado

with his parents; it was completely unlike Asher to do such a thing. The longer the phone went without ringing, the more convinced they were that the kids were truly up to no good.

At the end of Thursday afternoon, as the phone remained silent except for the Steak House ordering extra dinner rolls for their Friday night prime rib special, Edward and Penny offered once more for Lilly to join them at the house.

Lilly declined. She didn't know for sure what she would do at home, but she sure as heck wasn't going to spend any more time pondering the whereabouts of their children. Lilly was moving beyond being worried. She was feeling duped and she was angry about it. If her daughter wanted to burn bridges before she took off for college, then so be it.

As a matter of fact, she thought, as she drove the few blocks to their house, she was going to be proactive about sending Bree on her way. She was going to spend the evening packing up Bree's summer clothes and shoes. She wouldn't need the clothes she had left behind for Seattle in the fall, so Lilly would get a head start.

The more angry she became, the more Lilly thought that perhaps the best thing that could happen to both of them would be for Bree to leave for the University. An empty nest might be quite refreshing if her daughter was going to act like a complete imbecile.

Lilly was in the basement collecting Rubbermaid containers for Bree's belongings when the phone rang. Her first thought was, "Thank God, she's finally calling to tell me she's okay." Then she saw the caller I.D. It was a St. Louis area code. It had been ages since she'd heard from

57

Milt. She tried to remain calm as she answered.

"Hello?" Lilly answered as confidently as she could.

"Lillian? Is that you, young lady?"

"Hi, Milt. Yes, it's me." Lilly was on edge, waiting for the old man to say what he was calling for.

"You sound different—sort of hollow or something. Listen, girlie, I was calling to see how that granddaughter of mine is doing. She must have just graduated, didn't she?"

"Yes, Milt, she did. Two months ago, in fact."

"She there? If she is, you could just hang up to signal 'yes.' I don't want to cause any trouble, you know."

Lilly suddenly detected a hint of a slur. She relaxed. So that was what this phone call was about. Bree had not found him, like she feared. He was simply a little tipsy and reminiscing. That was often what brought him to call Lilly—that and loneliness.

"As a matter of fact, she is not here. She is out with friends tonight. How are you feeling these days? Well, I hope."

"Oh, you know me, Lillian. I'm plugging along like I always have. I was just turning in for the night and I started missing my little blond girl again. Do you think you could just send me a picture some time? I would keep it safe. I just want to see her again, before I die. It would do this old man a world of good."

"Milt, the day you leave this world, I will eat crow. I swear you are going to outlive all of us. That is if you don't drown yourself in that bottle of scotch you have on the desk in front of you."

"You know me too well, girlie. Just think about a picture, will you? It's been all of these years. If I didn't

58

have that picture of my big-eyed cherub of a granddaughter blown up on my fireplace mantle, I might forget entirely what she looked like."

"I can't stay on the phone with you, Milt. Just imagine if one of the help heard you talking to me. They might open their mouths to Dev. Then we really would be in a heap, wouldn't we? Get some rest and I'll be in touch, okay?"

"Okay, I'll be good for tonight and do as you ask. Lillian?"

"Yes, Milt?"

"I can't forget. You know that, don't you? Even after all of these years, I still ache to see both of you. Indulge this poor old man, will you?"

"I can't forget either. I've done my best, Milt, but our baby is all grown up now. Even if I indulge you, she may never know enough to do the same."

"I know Lillian. And that's the way it has to be. I understand. You give her a kiss for me."

"I'll do that when I see her."

"Good girl. Good night."

"Good night." And with that, Lilly cut the line to the one person who could knowingly link her to her complicated past. She couldn't help it. She just felt so sorry for Milton Devon, Sr., and she'd never had the heart to cut him off completely. He'd been discreet and he'd always been somewhat necessary, so he knew more than almost anyone about her.

In fact he knew more about her than BreeAnn ever would, if she had anything to say about it.

*

Bree hung up the phone in frustration. It was still busy.

She had tried five minutes ago, too. For the life of her, she would never understand why her mother wouldn't get call-waiting. Nonnie and Asher had already talked to their parents. They were ready to leave the diner and go to their campsite at the Topeka KOA. All that was holding them up was Bree and her mother's busy phone.

"Forget it, guys. I don't know who she's talking to, but I don't want to wait around all night until she hangs up. Your mom and dad will tell her we're okay."

"And that we're in California, like we said," Nonnie added.

"Do you really think they'll buy that?" Bree wasn't sure.

"Well since our parents wouldn't invest in caller ID and your mom wouldn't get call-waiting, then I'd say that worked out perfectly," Asher reassured Bree.

They were tired and anxious to turn in for the night. It had been a very long, very flat drive from North Platte to Tulsa. They hadn't been on the road nearly as long as they had the day before. But they all agreed that the flat, straight highways and endless cornfields of Nebraska and Kansas made the trip seem twice as long.

Besides that, they hadn't slept very well the night before.

The storm had let up at around four in the morning. Bree knew because she looked at her Indiglo watch every half hour or so during the night. Between paranoia that the overwhelming thunder was going to flatten their shelter, the soaking wet sleeping bag that had absorbed the groundwater under their tent, and her confused feelings about Asher and returning to St. Louis, Bree was unable to fall back to sleep.

Asher must have been quite awake, also, because as soon as the rain stopped, he had immediately pulled on a pair of jeans and left the tent. They had all grumbled and moaned while they took down their tent and hung out their bedding. They'd all put on dry clothes and took off to the nearest diner for an early breakfast. They had lost half of the day just waiting for their sleeping bags to dry out.

It turned out to be a blessing for Bree because she had gotten time to explore Cody Park too. She admired the peacocks and the white caribou and laughed at and envied all the little kids who played carefree on the playground. She explored all corners of the park, trying to jostle a memory from her babyhood visit to the place. She came up empty-handed. Was it all just a big mistake? Was it all a lie? Were they making this journey for nothing?

If it weren't for Asher and Nonnie and their constant reassurance and support, Bree would have turned back that Thursday. Instead, when their things were dry, they all got in the car and continued on. There were a few points of interest between Nebraska and Kansas. Because corners were so few and far between, they actually marked them with big yellow signs and arrows, even though they barely amounted to a bend in the otherwise straight road. There were no such warning signs in Washington where windy roads were the norm.

Also, none of them had ever seen oil being drilled before and they got to see several rigs on their way through Kansas. They looked like huge black grasshoppers dipping their mouths into the sienna-colored earth.

They had gotten to Topeka at about five. It was a beautiful capital city, rising up out of the plains. It was surprising in its historic flavor and mid-western hospitality. They had done a little sight-seeing, driving around the city a bit, before having dinner and calling home.

Now, though, Bree was exhausted and she was anxious. She was facing perhaps the biggest day of her life tomorrow. St. Louis was merely another five hours away. She had her father's physical address and the hope that he would be home on a Friday afternoon. She didn't know what she would say, and she had no idea what he would do. BreeAnn was about to step out of her life as she knew it and into the life of the lost little girl, Beatrice.

Bree shrugged and got in the car with Asher and Nonnie. If her mom hadn't been on the phone when she called, then Bree could have done as she promised and kept in touch. As it was, her mom was out of luck. Pateros was a whole lifetime away from what she was about to do and her mom was part of that. Perhaps she'd give her mom another chance to grill her when she had enough information to know if Lilly would tell the truth in return.

CHAPTER TEN

Asher had gotten on Google.com to get maps from Pateros to St. Louis. That leg of the trip had been relatively easy. What amazed Bree, the navigator for this leg, was that the list of directions from the edge of St. Louis proper to her father's home on Westminster Place was two-thirds of a page long.

Up until Friday, the trio had been able to avoid urban sprawl almost entirely. Topeka was a larger city, but in a small-town kind of way. They had stuck to the freeway through Kansas City. A city the size of St. Louis was daunting to these small-town kids. It began with suburbs too numerous to count. It continued through neighborhoods that looked historical, but seedy with age and neglect.

They were heartened to find that their journey through the Central West End of town revealed nicer brick and marble restorations and revitalized antique shopping areas. They turned onto Westminster, going through stately marble gates, and found an impressive row of brick and masonry mansions set back from the street and fronted by a well-coifed ribbon of greenery. Asher shook his head.

"How could they build these gorgeous, huge homes and make them so close together?" He asked.

"These look really old. Maybe back then it was easier to live in a neighborhood all together like this," Nonnie replied.

"Maybe it started with one wealthy family building a

home that was big enough to fill up an entire city lot, and then one neighbor after the other trying to outdo the size and snootiness of the last," she reasoned.

Bree was simply too nervous to guess. One of these historic old mansions was her father's house. They were moving slowly, looking at each house number until they pulled up in front of 4410. This was it.

How could it look so ordinary compared to the neighboring houses? She didn't know what she expected exactly. Perhaps that it would be painted blue instead of being red brick like everybody else's, that it might have a sign on it that said, "I've been missing my daughter for nearly seventeen years. Has anybody seen her?" Maybe she thought that a prominent doctor's house would just look different.

Nonnie and Asher looked at Bree expectantly. She was staring, pale-faced, suddenly not the confident, smart, fun-loving friend they both grew up with. She was about to bridge two lives: the one that she had lived and the one that she was supposed to live, but was denied.

Nonnie reached forward from the back seat and said gently, "This is it, Bree. Would you like me to go with you?"

"I'll go too, Bree, if you want me to," Asher added.

"I'd like to have you there, Nonnie, please," Bree answered shakily.

"Let's go then."

"Do we just knock on the door, do you think?" Bree was unsure of the etiquette involved. Nonnie nodded and they both took a deep breath.

There was a brass knocker and Bree lifted it heavily and knocked three times. A woman answered. She had skin black as night and curious, round hazel eyes that looked like they would be quick to smile. She was tiny, her body enveloped in an oversized maid's outfit. Aside from her non-descript clothing, she was the most exotic-looking woman Bree and Nonnie had ever seen.

"May I help you?" She asked the two girls, patiently, her voice smooth as the dark chocolate of her skin. They unfortunately had frequent solicitors in this area, so Dr. Devon often asked her to answer the door along with her other household duties. These two didn't look like your usual girl-scouts or brush-salesmen, however.

"Is this where Dr. Milton Devon lives?"

"Yes, this is his private home. What can I help you with without disturbing the good doctor?"

"Is he home?" Bree tried to look past the waifish woman.

She centered herself in the doorway, her patience wearing out. "Maybe if you told me what your business was, I would see if he was home or not."

"Well you must know if he's home….." Bree began to argue.

Nonnie interrupted. "I think he would be very interested in seeing my friend, here."

"Who *are* you?"

Bree was suddenly contrite, realizing that this woman may just shut the door on them before she even had a chance to explain why she was here.

"Can I ask what your name is, ma'am?" She asked politely.

"It's Carlotta. I work for Dr. Devon. Now it's your turn to answer my question."

"Carlotta, have you ever heard Dr. Devon speak of a

long-lost daughter by the name of Beatrice?"

Carlotta had heard the name many times. She knew that it was somewhat of an obsession of Dev Devon's. He had been trying to find Beatrice for years. Suddenly she stilled as she looked at the blond-headed girl closer. Then she quickly shut her mouth, as she realized that she must have been gaping. She had only seen that kind of hair on a few other people: Benjamin Devon and Dr. Milton Devon, Jr. himself.

"God Almighty," Carlotta exclaimed. "Forgive me. I saw you a few minutes ago, but I only just now really looked. Are you really her, honey?"

"I think so," Bree replied uncertainly.

"It's a miracle!" Carlotta began tearing up, then she smiled a huge, welcoming smile. "Well, don't just stand there, girl. Come in. Dr. Devon is home and so is your brother, Benjamin, and I just can't wait to go tell them the news."

Carlotta hurried away, her hosiery swishing with her quick steps. The next person who appeared had to be Bree's brother. Nonnie stifled a gasp as he appeared on the sweeping entrance staircase. If you put Bree's eyes and hair on a guy, this was what he would look like. He had it spiked and sticking straight up off the top of his head and he was, like a typical teenage kid, acting cool, though Bree could see the excitement brimming under his façade. He had heard them with Carlotta.

She was about to ascend the staircase to greet him when her father rushed into the room from the back of the house, looked her up and down a few times, and then invited her coolly into his office.

66

Nonnie followed, though he didn't directly invite her. He looked at her disapprovingly as he turned to close the door. Nonnie returned his look with an insolent glare. How could he be so aloof? Bree was his long-lost daughter, for goodness sake.

He pulled chairs to his desk for both girls. Then he sat across from them. Milton Devon, Jr., enthroned in his cherry wood-paneled office was an intimidating figure. His dark moss eyes were stern, assessing. His clothing was impeccable, an expensive navy suit jacket with a pinstriped tie and a yellow cotton dress shirt. He had his white-blond hair combed over to the side to hide an obvious bald spot. Bree shuddered to think that this was her father. Her mother was one of the warmest, most down-to-earth people in the whole world. How could she ever have been in love with this man?

"So you believe that you are Beatrice Devon, do you?"

"I think so, sir," Bree was automatically formal. His demeanor demanded nothing less.

"What leads you to believe this?"

"Just look at her, Dad!" His son interrupted from the doorway. "She looks just like me, only she's a girl."

"Don't interrupt, Benjamin. I can see that she looks a lot like us, but you must understand. I always thought that any return of my daughter would come from the authorities. I can't fathom how Beatrice could just show up on my doorstep after nearly seventeen years. There has to be some other explanation."

"It wasn't that hard to find you, sir. I found out where I was last seen and then I searched for everything else on the Internet," Bree was quietly insistent, not wanting to upset the man more than he already was.

"Okay, then. Where were you last seen?" Her father quizzed.

"North Platte, Nebraska. We went through there on the way here."

"So you came from the West. Where exactly did you leave from?"

Bree paled as she realized how easily she could have given up her mom's location, just by talking about the places they visited.

Nonnie interrupted, defending her confused friend. "Where we came from isn't really important. The point is that we came so that Bree, uh Beatrice, could find her father. Funny, but you don't seem all that happy to see her."

Dr. Devon scowled. He wished again that he could have talked to the blond without her rude friend. "Tell me more about how you found me, young lady," he continued.

"I came across a flier from the Center for Missing and Exploited Children. They must be like parents of kidnapped kids—they never really stop looking. I knew it was me in the picture because I had another baby picture to compare it to."

"I need more proof than that. There were several other girls over the years that made the same claims. You may know the drill—rich, prominent doctor, missing daughter, loads of money, society connections. Wouldn't it be great to belong to such a family?"

"What can I do to prove it to you? I left the pictures at home."

"Not that it would do any good. For all I know you could have stolen them. The proof lies on my little girl's sweet little second toe. The right foot—she had an oblong-shaped cherry-red birth mark on that tiny toe."

"It's on the left foot though, isn't it Bree?" Nonnie asked coyly.

Dev Devon fell suddenly still. His defensive, obnoxious demeanor fell away like an invisible cloak. It had been a test. Could it really be her?

Bree slipped her left foot from her clog. She had never liked showing her toes, because the brightly-colored birth mark drew attention.

Riveted, Milton Devon and his son, Benjamin watched her. She removed her anklet sock and brushed away a bit of lint from her foot. There was no mistaking it. She was Beatrice Devon.

Bree and Nonnie had never seen a man dissolve into tears before. But that is exactly what Bree's father did. He sat weakly in his stately office chair and wept like a baby. Benjamin was crying too as he hugged his older sister and then held her hand as they watched their father try to regain control over his emotions.

It took about five minutes, but once he had composed himself, he finally rose and embraced Bree warmly.

"I am so sorry to have put you through that, dear. I just had to know. I hope you understand…Welcome home, Beatrice. Welcome home."

And with that he smiled a wet, timorous smile and took Bree's other hand and kissed it and then tucked her arm in his to welcome Beatrice back to his home one room at a time.

CHAPTER ELEVEN

Dr. Dev Devon was charismatic as he showed Bree and Nonnie around. He had a beautiful, historic home. He would stop his chattering every once in a while to stop and stare at Bree. It made her uncomfortable, but it was somewhat understandable since he hadn't seen her in so long. It was as if he was trying to fill in the absence of her face for so long by memorizing her features now.

Bree wasn't really sure how to feel. Mostly she just felt numb. At least her father believed her now, but she just felt like it was all too weird—like she was in a badly scripted movie, only she didn't know the lines. She was improvising.

She could tell that her father was charming, but that he could be cruel. After all, she'd seen evidence enough of that downstairs. He was obviously wealthy and confident. Bree would need to get to know him better to know if she truly liked him or not. Wasn't she supposed to love her father instantly? She didn't know how she could do that with a complete stranger.

At least her brother was cute. If she judged correctly, he was about sixteen, which would have meant that her mother left him behind when he was just a tiny baby. Bree had just assumed that her brother would be older than she. She couldn't fathom how her mother could leave behind a newborn child, her own son, no less. But then there were obviously a lot of things she didn't know about Lilly.

Benjamin seemed to be a nice kid, though. Unlike many teenagers, Bree knew, Benjamin seemed eager to please, not aloof or apathetic at all. Two things were instantly clear about him: He was thrilled to know that he had his sister back and he was afraid of their father.

It took a mere glance or raised eyebrow from Dev to silence Benjamin. Benjamin tried a few times to share stories about their century-old house as he accompanied them on their tour. Dev tolerated it and when it seemed his son was stealing some of his thunder, he would send a silent censure. After about the third time this happened, Benjamin gave up.

He volunteered to go and get Asher when he learned that Nonnie's brother was still in the car. Bree sensed immediately that Nonnie and Asher were only marginally welcome here. Dev graciously invited them to stay for supper and he showed them to a room where they could stay together for the night. Bree found it objectionable that they should have to share a guest room when there were so many rooms to choose from, but it wasn't her place to question the owner of the house.

It was also made abundantly clear that Asher and Nonnie would be invited to return from where they came in the morning. Beatrice, of course, would be staying.

In all this cordiality, the unanswered questions that Bree and her father had for each other hung so thickly in the air that they all could have suffocated. But neither was of the nature to get that all out in the open. They were going to continue to get acquainted without talking about the past and what brought them both to this place.

Asher and Nonnie came from a family that held nothing back. They both wore their emotions on their sleeves. Suddenly Nonnie understood that quality about her best friend all that much better. Her dad was the same way. Only the people very closest to either of them would ever know them well enough to see past the façade they erected.

Though it exasperated them, Asher and Nonnie went along pretending they were just visitors from out of town. At dinner they discussed St. Louis and what the city had to offer. They talked about the weather. They talked about Benjamin's school—he went to a Catholic high school in the heart of the city and would be returning as a senior in the fall.

Bree held back telling them about her college plans and they did not ask, though her father must surely have known she'd already graduated. They never talked about home, though Dev Devon would hang on every word about their trip, trying to glean details about Beatrice's whereabouts for all of these years.

Carlotta, in the meantime, hung around after her housecleaning duties to help the cook cater to their guests. Neither of them was used to such excitement or turmoil. Normally it was just Benjamin and Dr. Devon, a late-night meal laid out and eaten in silence. That was if they were both home at the same time, which was rare.

Dr. Devon mentioned his thriving psychiatric practice. It turned out to be unusual that he would be home on a Friday afternoon. Normally his patients kept him at the hospital sometimes sixty or seventy hours in a week. He had skipped out that Friday, playing a round of golf in the morning and returning just in time to meet his long-lost daughter. Dev didn't much believe in fate, but he was sure glad burnout had led him to be home at the right time.

After dinner, Dev invited them all out to the veranda

behind the house. Despite the close neighbors, the high fence surrounding the small concrete and red-brick yard offered a modicum of privacy. It turned out that all the neighbors had a similar arrangement. His backyard was almost as private as Bree's at home. They drank minted iced tea and continued to make small talk.

Bree noticed that Benjamin spent a lot of time chatting up Nonnie. She couldn't really blame him. After all, Nonnie *was* gorgeous and interesting to talk to. She had often envied her friend's easy-going nature.

Bree also noted Asher's brooding silence in the corner chair of the patio table. He was either very interested in the flowered pattern on the tablecloth or he was trying very hard to avoid conversing with the others. Asher seemed angry. Bree could only imagine why.

Later, Bree returned to the bedroom that had once been her nursery. It was eerily undisturbed since her childhood. The only change since her absence had been the addition of a four-poster canopy bed, lined with wispy curtains and covered in a pink gingham comforter that matched the sun-faded curtains.

The closet was still brimming with toys. A wooden toy chest was at the foot of the bed. Bree shuddered when she opened the bureau drawer and realized that her toddler-sized clothes still filled the drawers. It was obvious that she had always been expected to return home, someday.

When a child dies, the parents initially cling to the things that belonged to that child. Sometimes it takes years, but they usually purge themselves of his or her things. Bree realized that a kidnapped child must bring a very different sort of grief. There would always be the hope that the child would return. There would never be any resolution, any rational way to move on with life.

This was her room, still. It was too bad that she remembered nothing about it. She had been trying all afternoon and evening to jog some memory, to excite some familiarity with her surroundings. Shouldn't her babyhood memories have some deep seat somewhere in her mind? If they did, they certainly weren't surfacing.

It was all strange and new and scary. She desperately wanted to keep Nonnie and Asher with her as long as possible, but her father had made it clear that they were not welcome to stay. He wasn't rude about it. He just continually referred to their departure the next morning as if it were the most natural thing in the world for them to drop off his long-lost daughter and make a quick exit.

Bree was pretty sure he didn't see why they would need to stay. They had done their duty and dropped her off. Their usefulness to him had worn off.

It was about eleven o'clock and Bree was still lying wide-eyed, unwilling and unable to shut off her thoughts, when she heard a soft scratch at the door. It was followed by Asher's silent entry into the room. Bree was facing toward the door. Asher rounded the bed and sat on its opposite side.

He could see in the dim glow of the pink nightlight that she was awake. She was breathing far too quickly to be asleep.

"How are you doing, Bree?" Asher murmured.

Bree whispered back. She had to be quiet. It would never do for her father to find a boy in her bed on her first night home.

74

"I'm terrible. I can't sleep. I don't want you and Non to leave." A tear slipped off her cheek as she started to voice her feelings.

"We don't want to leave either. It just about makes me ill to think about leaving you right now. Nonnie feels the same way."

"I'm just not sure there's anything we can do about it. I don't want to make my father angry. I just met him. It is his house."

"There's something not right about him, Bree."

"He's different from people back home, Asher. For one thing, he has money, lots of it. There aren't many people in Okanogan County who live like this. For another, he's like me. He avoids confrontation. He's hard to get to know. But I can tell that he's brilliant."

"He's really insensitive if he won't let us stay around a little longer for your sake."

"I keep wondering what my mother saw in him all of those years ago. I just can't for the life of me, make the connection."

"They are very different, aren't they." Asher laid himself full-length of the bed, getting closer so he could speak more quietly and so that he could be closer to Bree for perhaps the last time.

Bree was aware of Asher's nearness. Her response was to roll herself into his arms. She didn't care if her father found them. She needed to be close to her friends right now. If Nonnie was asleep, then Asher would have to do.

Asher ran his fingers through Bree's soft hair as she began to sob quietly on his t-shirt clad shoulder. He kissed her forehead.

"Shh, Bree. It's gonna be okay. After all, he is your

dad. He's half of you, so he can't be all bad."

"I know, Asher, but it's just that I feel so far from home. I don't want you to leave and then I want to leave with you. If I turned my back on all of this, though, I might never learn who I really am.

"I'm terrified because I know that my mom took me from here suddenly. She must have had a good reason and I intend to find out what that was. But, what happens if I don't like the answer?"

"You are such a brave girl, Bree. You will find the answers and home will always be there. Just promise me one thing."

"What?" Bree sniffled, all dignity gone, wiping her nose on her own t-shirt.

"Don't tell him where you've been. He's going to pressure you to tell him. He may even try to charm it out of you. But you can't tell him, Bree. You know that, right?"

"Right. Because he might come after Mom."

"From what I've seen, Bree, I know that he would. He could be ruthless. I don't want Lilly or any of us back home to be hurt by this. Maybe that's selfish, but I'm sure you can see why."

"I don't want any of you hurt either. Maybe in that way it's best that you and Nonnie get away from here. I'm sure he won't harm me, but I don't know about anyone else. I need something from you too, Asher."

"You name it, Bree."

"You can't tell Mom where I am. I'll call and reassure her that I'm okay, but I'm not ready to tell her that I'm here yet. Perhaps by the time you get home, I will have worked things out."

"What should I tell her? She'll never buy that we just

left you behind."

"Tell her that I've fallen in love and that I refused to leave his side."

Asher smiled. "That's a pretty tall tale, but if Nonnie and I embellish on it all the way home, it should be passable."

Bree laughed lightly, thinking of the expression on her mother's face when she found out her eighteen-year-old daughter had become someone's love slave.

"It's almost too cruel!" She exclaimed.

"But it'll be a fun story to tell. Much better than telling her we've delivered you into your father's hands."

Bree grew serious. "It won't be entirely untrue, Asher, the part about me falling in love."

"How so?"

"I have fallen in love on this trip. I always knew that I loved Nonnie. She's my soul mate. But you, Asher. You make my heart fishtail. I don't know what else to call it. It must be love."

Asher didn't know how to respond. He was a little older than Bree. He knew the difference between love and lust. But he didn't just want her. He wanted to protect her. He wasn't sure if it was brotherly concern or if it was attraction. Maybe it was love, new and fragile love. All he knew was that they wouldn't have time to cultivate it. He didn't want to make it any harder on her when they left in the morning.

"Bree, you are so sweet and beautiful and I am honored that you feel that way about me. Let me make you a deal. If you come back and we both still feel the way we do now, then we'll try to figure it out."

"Then you'll wait for me?"

"I'll wait for you, Bree." With that, he gave her a chaste kiss and ruffled her hair one more time and slipped silently out of her room.

Bree finally let her eyes close.

CHAPTER TWELVE

Lilly stuck her head under the pillow after the phone's first shrill ring reverberated through the house. It was Saturday. What in the world was the phone doing ringing at five in the morning? Then she woke up suddenly. BreeAnn. She was finally calling her frazzled mother.

Lilly automatically checked the area code on the phone. It was Milt again. That was strange. He rarely called twice in such a short span of time. Lilly gathered her thoughts as she hit the talk button.

"Good morning, Milt."

"She's here, Lillian."

"Who's there, Milt? I'm sorry. It's just so early here. I haven't got my wits about me yet." Lilly's mouth was dry. She took the cordless with her to the kitchen, her full-length satin nightgown swishing in the early morning silence.

"Our girl, Lillian. She's here. In St. Louis."

Lillian had picked up a tumbler. That was a mistake. It fell into the sink with a crash as Lilly's blood stood still.

"Lillian, dear, are you there? What was that horrible crash? Are you all right?"

It took a few moments for Lilly to breathe. When her air returned, she began to hyperventilate.

"Calm down, dear. Really. She's okay. In fact, according to Dev, she's wonderful. He's thrilled to see her again, as you can imagine," Milt rambled on, trying to calm Lilly's obvious panic.

"Lillian, you must breathe. Really, woman, get a grip," Dr. Milton Devon, Sr. used his most authoritative voice.

Lilly tried hard to do just that, taking a few deep gulps of air.

Milt continued, "I'm going to see her later this morning, Lillian. Dev has invited me for a late brunch. He really must be feeling elated. We haven't spoken in ages. Our relationship, as you know, has been strained over the last several years. He actually wants me to see Beatrice, now that she's home again."

The gears in Lilly's mind began to shift once again. Dev had Bree. How in the world had Bree found him? This trip of hers had been a guise to find her long-lost father. If only Bree knew what a mistake it would be to let Dr. Dev Devon back into her life.

"Has Dev shared where Beatrice ventured from? Does he know where I am, Milt?"

"He didn't say, dear, but that is the reason I called you. I don't know how Beatrice found him and I intend to ask, subtly, mind you, today. I am overjoyed at the thought of getting reacquainted with my granddaughter. I truly am. But I'm worried about you, Lillian. My son will never rest until he finds you and punishes you for taking his daughter away all of these years."

"I'm aware of that, Milt. My life and Bree's life, as we knew it, is over. That's what you are telling me."

"I am afraid so. Do what you need to do and please do it soon. Trust that I will help you. You need only to tell me how."

"You need to tread carefully too, Milt. Never let on that you helped me all of those years ago. Dev would be just as quick to punish you if he knew."

"Yes, he would."

"Now, go Milt and give our girl a kiss for me. It will all work out. Don't worry about me, really."

"Okay, Lillian. Be strong and please keep me informed."

"Goodbye, Milt." And with that, Lilly hung up the phone. It was strange how peaceful the early morning pall settled once again as she became quiet. After all, it seemed fitting that the dawn should have shattered into chaos along with the rest of her life.

Bree was a mess waiting for brunch to come and go because that was when she would have to face the inevitable and let Nonnie and Asher leave. She'd also learned earlier that morning that her paternal grandfather, Dr. Milton Devon, Sr., would be joining them.

If Dev Devon was imposing, imagine how his father might be, Bree thought as she dressed casually in an olive-colored t-shirt and white shorts. The shirt brought out the dramatic green of her dark eyes. It was too bad that they were rimmed in shadows this morning. She would have to dab on some concealer to disguise the obvious lack of sleep.

She joined Asher and Nonnie in the hall and they all proceeded downstairs to breakfast as if they were on a death march. Asher had already packed he and Nonnie's stuff in the car. They would leave directly after their meal.

Bree's grandfather was waiting in the foyer. Whatever Bree had expected of him, he defied completely. His eyes were sea blue and dancing with happiness. He had a shock of "feathers" on his head very much like her own. She

81

could see that the humidity of Missouri wasn't any kinder to his coif than it was to hers. Unlike Dev Devon, who had plastered his unruly hair to his head, the elder Devon had his cut very short and it spiked around his head, giving him a white-streaked, Rod Stewart look.

He was dressed in wrinkled old khakis, a half-tucked red polo, and navy blue boat shoes. He looked like he'd been sailing. In fact, he had been walking. He lived three miles to the north of Dev and he had hiked them. It was a beautiful summer day, after all.

Before Bree even had time to think about stopping him, Milton Devon, Sr. enveloped his granddaughter in a bear hug. There were tears in his eyes as he let go. Then he grabbed his grandson, Benjamin and hugged him too. He ruffled Benjamin's hair.

"It's been a long time, squirt," his grandfather teased. It was clear that Benjamin loved his grandpa and was truly glad to see him.

Dev Devon watched all of this with a certain detachment. He scowled at his father's unkempt attire. You'd think he was a transient the way he dressed. And he had a perfectly good Lincoln. Why he had to walk everywhere was beyond Dev's comprehension.

He noticed that Beatrice looked tired. She was also dressed awfully casually for a Saturday brunch. He would have to teach her the fashion requirements of a young woman of her stature in the community. People would expect a certain amount of class from his daughter. If she didn't possess it yet, he would see to it that she learned.

If she was raised by his liberated bitch of a sister-in-law, as he suspected she was, then Beatrice was entirely faultless if sophistication escaped her. Lillian had not one

82

iota of class as far as he was concerned.

Dev put the hateful thoughts aside. There would be enough time for revenge later. For now he wanted to focus on reacquainting himself with his daughter. Once he fed and dispensed of her clingy friends, then he could get to the business of knowing her better.

Breakfast was eaten quietly with none of them willing to engage in the same kind of small-talk that had reigned the night before. Only Milt kept the conversation moving, asking Nonnie and Asher about their Native American heritage and inquiring about Benjamin's upcoming school activities. It turned out that Benjamin was quite accomplished at debate, a subject that Milton Devon, Sr. had also enjoyed very much.

Soon their meal was over and Bree said a tearful goodbye to her friends. She put on a brave face, though, the minute they drove away. It was time to encounter her family. She had some questions and it was time to get some answers.

By the time she stepped back inside, Dev had gone to the kitchen to make plans with Grace, the cook, for dinner. Milt took the opportunity to sweep Beatrice into the den for a moment.

"How are you doing, Beatrice, really? You seem rather in shock for all of this."

"I am a little out of my comfort zone, here. Should I call you grandfather or Milton, or what would you prefer?"

"You can call me 'Grandpa' when you're comfortable with it. I don't expect that you will, right away, though."

"Okay."

"I called Lillian, this morning, Beatrice. You haven't called her since you arrived, have you?"

"How do you know how to get a hold of her?" Bree was shocked that her grandfather might have known her whereabouts all of these years.

"Let's just say that I've been necessary to you both. Now, dear, Dev has no idea, so you must never let on that I've known anything about you."

"Okay, Grandfather. Since you know what's going on, though, I have one burning question for you."

"What's that, honey?"

"Why did my mom kidnap me?"

"Your *mom*?" Milton Devon was confused. Then he realized. Maybe Lillian hadn't told her everything. In fact, she may have told her absolutely nothing about her past.

"Oh dear, I assumed that you knew," he lamented.

Bree was alarmed. "Knew *what*?"

"Beatrice, dear, your mom didn't kidnap you at all. Lillian is your aunt."

CHAPTER THIRTEEN

At hearing this newest revelation, BreeAnn burst into tears and ran from the room, nearly knocking a Roman bust from its mahogany stand, shoving past her shocked father who had just arrived in the doorway of the den. Dev steadied the sculpture and turned an accusing glare toward his father.

"What in the world was that about? Are you upsetting your only granddaughter already when you've only just been reintroduced?"

"Well, I'm sure I don't know," Milton Devon was sure to tread carefully here. He didn't want Dev finding out about Lillian, though he was almost certain he would have his people looking for her. The only reason the cavalry wasn't already headed to Washington was that Dev hadn't had enough time to quiz Beatrice. In time, Milton was certain that he would and then it was only a matter of hours before Lillian would be in great danger.

"Perhaps she was just overwhelmed by emotion, as I was at first."

Dev's eyes narrowed. His father was hiding something. Dev bristled, then he relaxed. It was okay. Smooth-talking Dev could ferret information out of anybody. His father had never been able to stand up to it.

"Seems to me like that would have come before brunch. What did you say to her?"

Milton thought as fast as his old brain would allow

him. If only he could have a slip of scotch. That would clear him up. He paused for a moment, then offered, "I only told her that she looked wonderful and that her mother would be overjoyed to see her again."

The words hit their mark. Dev couldn't tolerate any discussion of his wife, Beatrice's mother.

"You never change do you, Father? Why would you have to go bringing up Shannon now? She's not even here. It's not like she's going to be significant to Beatrice."

"Surely you're going to let her see her own daughter. Despite her illness, Dev, she must miss Beatrice terribly. Heaven couldn't take away the mother-child bond."

"Shannon wouldn't know Beatrice from any other teenager. She's completely unable to comprehend or communicate."

"Dev, you and I are both psychiatrists. I know, as well as you do, that we are completely unable to know what Shannon does and does not understand. You are correct that she doesn't communicate, but what happens when she lays eyes on her own child, the child that came from her womb, whom she hasn't seen for almost seventeen years? She may have a complete breakthrough. That would be a blessing for your whole family, you and Benjamin included."

"You forget, Father. She has done that many times. Benjamin goes to visit her on occasion, with me. She doesn't respond to us. What makes you think that she would respond to Beatrice?"

"Just a hunch, Son. That's all."

"At any rate, you need to leave Shannon and all of that business up to me. It's really none of your concern. I should think we've had enough disagreement where she's concerned. I've invited you over to move past all of that.

"Beatrice is home, Father," Dev continued. "That is what we are going to concentrate on—knowing her again," Dev stared his father down, until he looked away. That was good. Dev had gotten his point across. He changed the subject.

"Beatrice looks beautiful, don't you think? She's gotten her looks from our side. She seems healthy and happy and well-adjusted. It's surprising, considering the violent separation she must have suffered when she was a baby." Dev lit his customary after-meal cigarette.

Waving away a curl of smoke, Milton coughed lightly and frowned his disapproval. Beatrice, he thought, *had* turned out well, thanks to Lillian. "She is a lovely girl. She seems tired, though. Perhaps she can get some rest while she's here. I'm sure that you will see that her needs are met."

"Absolutely. I should probably go check on her and make sure that she wasn't too upset by your mention of her mother. You are welcome to come visit Beatrice anytime, Father. It is good to see you again. Just try to be a little more sensitive with her next time, will you?"

Milton knew when he was being dismissed. Besides, his lungs were burning from the tobacco-polluted air. It was about time for him to make the trek back to his home.

"Think about what I said regarding Shannon, Dev."

"Leave it, Father. I won't discuss it with you. Be careful walking home. Try to avoid the Park area. I've heard there are some undesirables making trouble for pedestrians."

"I'll keep that in mind." Milton set out toward Forest Park anyway. No hoodlums were going to keep *him* from enjoying his Saturday hike.

Bree's room was at the top of the staircase. She ran as fast as she could up the stairs, slammed open the door to her room, and slammed it shut again. Maybe if she splintered some wood she would feel better. None of it gave way, so instead she sank to the pink shag floor to grieve the loss of the only mother she'd ever known.

The enormity of the lies she'd been told almost rivaled how long she had believed them. Lilly was her aunt, not her mom. For inexplicable reasons, Lilly had also kidnapped her when she was still a baby. The nearly seventeen years in Pateros, they weren't the ideal childhood years that she remembered, they were years spent as fugitives. They were years *taken* from her and from her real family.

Bree had lost everything. She didn't know her father, her real mother. Even her *name* wasn't her real name. Her real name was Beatrice. She didn't know or recognize Beatrice. How was she supposed to *be* her?

Then another thought broke through her angry haze. If Lilly wasn't her mother, then where was her real mother? She had thought she was going to St. Louis to meet just her father. If she had a mother, then where was she? Were she and her father divorced? Was she dead? Oh, God, she didn't want to think of that possibility.

What if her mother needed to see her as much as her father did? How would she possibly find her? All of the research they had done had led them here. What if her mother was somewhere else entirely? Would her father tell her? Could she trust him?

Oh, why did Asher and Nonnie have to leave? She had half a mind to go running after them. They would have to stop somewhere, after all. She knew the way back. Maybe she could catch up to them.

She was irrational, horrified, angry. And it was all her mother's, no her *aunt's,* fault. She was trying hard to reconcile the woman who had ruined her life with the loving, trusting, understanding mom that she grew up with.

It explained a lot of things, really. Like the fact that Lilly let very few people close to her—Bree had even found her enigmatic at times. It also explained why they had gone to such a far away, obscure place to make a new life, and why Lilly would never talk about the lifetime before. It explained the photographs, or the lack thereof.

At least her mom had told the truth about her having a father and a brother. Lilly also knew that they were alive and well and mere days away. Bree could see how her father might be some kind of bad guy, but Benjamin hadn't done anything to deserve losing his sister.

And her mother—Lilly tried hard to remember the name of the sister she had seen with Lilly in the hat box photos. What was it? Sheila? Sharon? Maybe it was Shannon. That sounded right. Bree had been wondering since the day before how her mom could have abandoned her baby boy. It turned out, however, that instead she had taken her niece and denied her sister and nephew a chance to know her.

It was downright baffling. Bree knew one thing, though. She needed to make a phone call. She dried her angry tears and freshened up in the bathroom across the hall. She would go to her father's study to use the phone. She had questions and it was long past time for her to check in, caller ID be damned. Lilly had better be ready to talk.

Dev listened outside the door while Bree cried. He wanted to offer comfort, an explanation for her mother's absence, but he didn't know how to approach her exactly. This Beatrice was a stranger. Besides, confession had never really been his thing.

He ducked into the stairwell when she stomped suddenly back to her door and exited with a red, tear-streaked face.

'Mustn't be seen eavesdropping,' he thought.

He continued down the stairs and went to his study to collect his thoughts. It was his favorite place to do so. To his surprise, Beatrice came barreling down the stairs just moments later. He smiled as he recognized the determined look on her face. She was headed his way.

"Um, Father, I wondered if I may be able to use your phone," she began, discomfited to find that the study was occupied. "I need to call, uh, someone important...."

"You needn't explain, Beatrice, dear," Dev interrupted. "You want privacy, is that it?"

She nodded.

"We'll have to see to it that you get your own phone at some point. You can have whatever you want. Do you know that? You need only to ask."

"Thank you, Father."

Dev left the study and closed the door discreetly. He went upstairs to his room, newly elated. This couldn't be more perfect! It would be mere hours before he had the information he so dearly wanted. His girl was about to call home. He would give her all of the privacy she needed, then he would find out where she called. Lillian's cover was about to be blown and Dev had a distinct advantage. She would pay, by God. Lillian would pay for everything.

CHAPTER FOURTEEN

By noon, Lilly was driving to Wenatchee to catch a
commuter flight to Seattle. She remained dry-eyed as she
drove away from her bakery and her very good friends.
Perhaps her sojourn in Pateros had been a complete lie,
but it had been years and years filled with success and
joy. After the first few years, she had really, truly stopped
looking over her shoulder.

Despite this, she did always have a plan should Dev
ever find her or Bree. She knew it would take Dev no
time at all to find out where she was once Bree was in his
clutches.

Her lawyer was in Omak. Despite the fact that it was
Saturday, Denise Reynolds knew that a call from Lilly
could come at any time. It had been a brief conversation.
The wheels were set in motion.

The bakery would have to be sold. It wouldn't,
however, ever make it to any real estate listings. Penny
would be the lucky new owner for the bargain price of fifty
dollars. Lilly had arranged such a buyout five years ago,
unbeknownst to Penny.

Lilly chuckled as she thought of the look of horror
Penny would have on her face when she found out that
Lilly had sold her the bakery and then realized that she
would have to do all of the baking herself for the next week
or two while she found a new baker. It would be bittersweet
for both of them, for sure. But Penny deserved the business.

She had helped build it.

Denise would also see to it that Lilly's house was sold and all of her valuables and Bree's, aside from what she could fit into two large suitcases, would be liquidated. Denise was also in charge of disconnecting all of Lilly's utilities and forwarding her mail to her own law office where she was allotted funds to pay any outstanding bills.

Lilly had set up bank accounts under the name Darcy White, her mother's maiden name. She had all of the identification she needed to assume the new identity. She had stuffed it in a solid green hat box on the shelf of her closet. She'd also had documents made for Bree, but she hadn't updated them since Bree was a child, thinking mistakenly that she might never need to hide with her niece again.

The beauty of the attorney-client privilege was that Denise needed never inquire or know about Lilly's reasoning. If she suspected criminal activities on Lilly's part, she never let on. Denise just made the arrangements and wished her client well.

Lilly was grateful that Denise had never probed, but she had been at the ready when Lilly called her. The two women had been unspoken friends and Lilly would feel forever indebted for Denise's quick help. She had needed a hasty exit, a head start on Dev Devon and she felt like she was getting it.

⊷━━▪━

The phone rang and rang. The machine didn't even pick up. The bakery was closed on Saturday, so Bree couldn't even imagine where Lilly might be. She supposed she may have made the trek North to Omak or to Wenatchee to catch up on shopping. Bree felt a pang as she realized that she would love to be there with her mom doing just that.

Anger flooded back as Bree remembered once again that Lilly wasn't her "mom" at all. She could really take her shopping and shove it, Bree thought furiously. Why wouldn't she ever just answer her phone anymore?

Bree slammed the phone down. She couldn't have known that Lilly was in the throes of fleeing just then. All she knew was that no one was around to give her answers anymore. She was completely on her own. It was scary, but she was a grown-up now, right?

Bree stuck her chin out and resolved once again to get the answers to her questions. She didn't know her father very well at all, but she was going to approach him anyway. He was her only accessible link to her past and she was just going to have to trust him for now.

Dev's master suite was indulgent in every way. The whole area was half as large as the second floor of his brick restoration. He had wanted it that way when he and Shannon did the work on the house. He had wanted their suite to be their apartment within their home so that when they had children, they would also have privacy.

It was too bad she'd been so ready to abandon it for her own simple room after they had Beatrice. It had been the beginning of her undoing when she left their marriage bed.

The door opened into a tasteful sitting room with silken wallpaper and cherry hardwood floors. The settee and sofa were of rich, blue brocade. Just past the sitting area, the room opened to the right to reveal a fully-stocked cocktail bar and two brocade-covered cherry barstools.

Past the wall of the sitting area was the actual bedroom. The bed was an enormous blend of cobalt blue silk and brocade, all surrounded by four posters of rich mahogany. To the far side was Dev's favorite leather chair and a sixty-five inch television and home theater. The voluminous bathroom and dressing area disappeared to the right beyond the theater area.

The carpet in the main bedroom was deep, white berber and Dev was studying its pattern intently when Bree knocked tentatively on the door, interrupting his reverie.

"Come in, please," he called.

"Father, I was wondering if I could ask you a few questions."

"Of course, anything you need, Beatrice, like I said. Were you able to make your telephone call okay?"

"Nobody answered."

Dev put a quick check on his disappointment. If there had been no answer, then it would be very difficult for him to track the call. He wasn't sure if it was even possible.

Bree thought she detected a trace of annoyance in her father's expression, but she couldn't be sure. That was strange. Maybe she was just mistaken.

"I want to know more about my mother. Grandpa mentioned her earlier today."

"Yes, he did, didn't he? I am so sorry if he upset you, Beatrice. He and I talked and it won't happen again, I assure you."

"I wasn't really that upset with him. It was just, well, I am going to have to tell you something about my childhood. I haven't up until now, because I didn't want my mom, I mean, um, my aunt to get in trouble."

Dev interrupted, "You mean to tell me that you think Lillian is your mom?"

"Well I did until Grandpa Devon set me straight."

"That no-good, child-stealing witch is not anything like your mother, Beatrice."

Bree was taken aback. He knew that Lilly had taken her, obviously. And it was easy to see that he wanted her to pay dearly for having taken precious Beatrice away. The hate registered in his eyes.

Bree jumped to Lilly's defense. "She did a good job bringing me up. Really. I have had an ideal childhood. She was a single mother and she was very good at it. I've trusted her so much that I didn't want to tell you where she was or where I came from because I want to protect her. And I will protect her, Father, just so you know."

Dev could see that determination surfacing again—so familiar, so amusing in its likeness to his own. He needed to leave this alone, he could tell. If he continued to berate Lillian, Beatrice would only draw further away. His training as a psychiatrist gave him an excellent ability to read people. He needed to cajole Beatrice some other way, win her trust, somehow.

"You want to know about your real mother, Beatrice?"

"Yes. More than anything," Bree replied, hopeful.

"Her name is Shannon Waters-Devon and she lives very near here in a hospital called St. Louis State Hospital."

Bree was alarmed, "Is she sick?"

"She has been ill for many years, Beatrice, since before you disappeared. The State Hospital is a mental institution."

Bree felt the bile rising in her throat. Why did she eat such a large breakfast? The emotional upset of this morning had continually brought forth her stomach's rejection of its myriad contents.

Her mom was crazy. That was what he was telling her. Bree sat down on the silken settee.

Not knowing if she really wanted to know, she asked anyway, "What's wrong with her?"

"Shannon had problems with post-partum depression after she had you. I thought we had the depression under control with medication and counseling. Shannon seemed happy, back on track. I was doing my very best to treat her.

"Then we had Benjamin just a year and half later. Two babies so close together just sent Shannon over the edge. She had a breakdown and, shortly thereafter, became catatonic. I had to put her in the hospital since I was too busy with my practice and a new baby to take care of her any longer. You were taken from us in the midst of all of this. I sometimes think that maybe Shannon would have recovered, had her trauma not been so great from losing you too."

"So, if I want to see her, would she know who I am?" Bree asked tearfully.

"I'm so sorry, Beatrice, dear, but I don't think so. Shannon hasn't responded to Benjamin either."

"I might want to see her anyway, Father. Do you think that I could do that?"

It broke Dev's heart to see Beatrice so worried about her mother. He might have to work out a visit. Surely that could be managed.

"I will see if we can do that. I promise. I don't want you to worry in the meantime, Beatrice. There was nothing you could do to prevent what happened. You were too little.

"Your aunt made Shannon's recovery impossible," he added. "You can understand why I'm so angry with her."

"I do understand, in a way. But I can't hate her."

"I know, Beatrice, but you might when you realize the enormity of what she's done to you and your family."

"I'm afraid you might be right," Bree replied. She sighed deeply.

"We can talk about all of this later. It's Saturday, do you realize that, Beatrice? I have a reservation for us for dinner at the Downtown Athletic Club. In the meantime, I want to show you a bit of St. Louis. We have this wonderful place called the Plaza Frontenac. If you don't mind, I would like to outfit my daughter properly for her role in St. Louis society. Do you like to shop, Beatrice, sweetheart?"

Bree saw through her misery long enough to see that this might be an opportunity to have some fun and to get to know her father a little better.

"What girl doesn't like to shop?" Bree asked, and she smiled tentatively as she took her father's extended arm. He led her happily to his silver Jaguar sedan for a tour of his beloved city. It was time to bestow upon Beatrice her birthright.

CHAPTER FIFTEEN

There were more outings over the course of the next week. St. Louis was a vibrant, historic city and Bree enjoyed seeing it from the perspective of a native. Tourists would frequent Lafayette Square and the St. Louis arch. Bree was shown these too. But she was also given tours of exclusive, private Lafayette Square homes that belonged to friends of her father.

She swam in the pool at the Downtown Athletic Club and played her first round of golf in Webster Groves. Instead of window-shopping at the Plaza Frontenac, she made like *Pretty Woman* and sat in a chair at Saks Fifth Avenue while a small army of clerks and salespeople waited on her. Bree walked out with the largest wardrobe of new clothes she had ever imagined, all accessorized and packed in bags too numerous to fit in her father's convertible.

Her father saw to it that her packages were delivered to the house. Dev Devon commanded respect and admiration and Bree found that she too had both whenever she accompanied him. She wasn't sure if it was his money or his attitude, but her father expected the treatment he was given. He also expected Beatrice to behave as he did. He called the behavior classy.

Behind his back, Bree and Benjamin called it snobby. Nevertheless, they both played along—Benjamin because he was used to it; Bree because she didn't know any better.

Bree was grateful when she had Benjamin at the house. It was a relationship they approached somewhat cautiously since neither was used to having a sibling. They made small talk and bantered about their father. They weren't really to the point of talking about themselves much.

Besides, Benjamin was a busy guy, doing all of the important things that a sixteen-year-old does. Bree found herself often at the mercy of her father because her brother was off doing something else.

Her father was intent on broadening Beatrice's palate. Over the course of the week, Bree tried caviar and cream cheese, escargot and Mississippi River Mussels, braised lamb and New England crab cakes.

Bree had never had veal before. One thing there was no shortage of in Okanogan County was calves frolicking about alongside every two-lane highway. The thought of eating a calf that had been birthed and confined and then butchered had never appealed to either Lilly or Bree. It sickened her actually. But Bree gave it a shot when her father insisted that she try it at dinner that first night. The Downtown Athletic Club had a world-renowned chef and she had to admit that the veal melted like butter in her mouth.

It was delicious when you made yourself forget what it was.

Bree had to admit that it was also fun to get dressed up on a regular basis. There was no end to the invitations they received for dinner. Dev had a whole line-up of suitable young men he was introducing Beatrice to, mainly so that if she decided to date, she would know the kind of companion he expected her to have. They were the sons of other doctors, graduates of prestigious Ivy League universities,

99

all born with a silver spoon and boring, predictable personalities.

She played along. This striking blond-haired young woman was a new prospect in St. Louis society. Their interest was piqued. Bree was funny and unspoiled. She was a small-town girl, refreshing. The young men noticed. Bree would entertain them and maintain a polite amount of distance also.

At night she dreamed of crashing thunder and glistening droplets on icy hot brown skin. She saw a flash of white, white teeth as the man of her dreams leaned in to kiss her.

In private, Bree mourned her best friends—Nonnie, who had been here with her for the biggest event of her life; and Asher, the man whose friendship was blossoming into so much more, unexpectedly and surprisingly swiftly. She wondered where they were, if they had arrived at home yet. Nonnie promised to call her when they did. As the days turned to a week, Bree wondered if they would ever call her again.

Asher and Nonnie took a full nine days to drive home from St. Louis. For one thing, neither of them had anywhere to be until mid-September. For another, they didn't want to face their parents any sooner than they had to. There would be hell to pay, this they were sure of. Besides, the states between Missouri and Washington were gorgeous and unexplored and they had plenty of money left since they'd been so conservative on the way down.

Bree had insisted they take the remaining money with them since she had her father's resources should she decide to go home. Asher hadn't been so sure. What if she had needed to leave on her own? After all, she didn't know what kind of a guy Dr. Devon was yet. Asher and Nonnie sure hadn't liked him. It was hard to believe that the same startling moss-colored eyes that had made Bree so warm and beguiling to Asher could make her father look so hard and calculating.

The two of them tried their best to forget leaving her behind, though it tore at the both of them to not have her around. They took a less direct route home, exploring the Black Hills of South Dakota and Mount Rushmore, spending a full four days at Yellowstone National Park, and driving through Northeastern Oregon for the first time.

They didn't call their parents. Keeping in touch had been Bree's promise, not theirs. They were adults. Edward and Penny would just yell at them. They would go home and face the music soon enough. They didn't want to make any confessions yet about where they'd been or what package they had delivered. This served two purposes: It gave Bree plenty of time to decide what to tell Lilly and to get to know her father; and it gave them time to enjoy each other before they had to grow up and go their separate ways.

It was with resignation that Asher steered into the town of Pateros from the south. It was a hot summer Monday afternoon. The pedestrian traffic was light as the few residents of the town were either at work or hiding from the blazing high desert sun. Asher was glad they had fixed the air conditioning in the car. The blast of heat that hit him when he opened the car door at the bakery was almost enough to knock him over. It was at least 100 degrees outside.

When he saw the expression on his mother's face, standing with her arms crossed just inside the glass door of the bakery, Asher knew that the intense heat was trivial. His mother was going to kill them.

"Nonnie, you stay here. I want to try and explain to Mom before you come in. She looks pissed."

"No way, Brother. We're in this together. Remember? We'll be stronger two against one."

"Yeah, except you need to check your three o'clock. Dad saw us from his shop. He's coming too," Asher swallowed nervously.

Nonnie took a deep breath and stepped out of the passenger side.

Edward ran up to them, red-faced, angry. The kids looked humbled, though, and their faces sad. Bree Ann wasn't with them, he knew. But he was grateful to see them. His resolve to punish them crumbled and the anger turned to soft tears as he embraced each of them silently. Asher was stiff, still worried about this reunion. Nonnie melted into his arms.

Penny was next to give them quick hugs, but she was not so ready to forgive.

"You two are gonna get it. Fortunately for you, I can't leave the bakery until six o'clock. So here's what's going to happen: Asher, you are going to drive this car straight home and park it. You are going to unpack it and lock it and put the keys on the kitchen counter. Nonnie, you are going to clean that filthy room you left behind. It's starting to smell.

"Asher, you are going to *walk* over to the quick stop and explain to your boss why you just ran out and left your job behind with no notice and then you are going to tell him how you're going to make it right. Now get going. We'll talk later at home. So help me, if you don't do these things, I will get violent. That is a promise."

Penny turned on her heel and marched back into the bakery.

Edward sighed. "It's good to have you home safe. Now, you'd better do what your mother says."

They nodded and got back into the car to go home.

Nonnie cleaned her room first. She only had three hours until her mom came home and her room really was a mess. She and Bree had been so busy planning that Nonnie hadn't paid attention to the cyclone that had hit her living space. She started a load of wash and filled an entire trash bag full. She even dusted and Windexed her mirror after putting her vanity in order.

She hurried to vacuum and finish because she wanted to have the opportunity to call Bree before Penny arrived home.

Asher had gone to the quick stop and returned red as a beet. His boss had actually been pretty cool. Asher agreed to take a pay cut of fifty cents and finish out the summer, working nights, which no one else wanted to do. Asher had apologized for leaving Bennie in a lurch and both of them felt pretty good when he left.

Then he walked home in the August late afternoon heat. The bank thermometer said that it was 105 degrees. Eastern Washington's heat, at least, was dry as a bone, but it also felt like it was drying off his sweat sooner than it could leave his pores. Asher was good and ready for a cold shower by the time he walked the quarter mile home.

He, too, wanted to be ready to call Bree before their

parents arrived home.

They called from Nonnie's room.

"Devon Residence," the smooth, warm voice of Carlotta answered.

"Hi, Carlotta. It's Nonnie. Remember me?"

"Of course. You have returned home safely, then?"

"We have. Asher is here too. Do you mind getting Bree, um, Beatrice for us? We promised to call her when we got home."

"I'll see if she's upstairs." Carlotta jotted down the number on the Caller ID. Dev Devon had asked her to do this should any calls come for Beatrice. It was a bit unusual, but she didn't blame him for wanting to know where her kidnapper had kept her for so long.

Nonnie and Asher waited. Bree came to the phone a few moments later. She sounded breathless from having run down the stairs to the study.

"Hi! Are you guys home? I thought you'd never call! I've got so much to tell you."

"You sound like you're doing okay, Bree. Are you?" Nonnie's first concern was her friend's well-being.

"I'm fine, Non. My father is sort of intimidating, isn't he? But his heart is in the right place, really. He's been spoiling the heck out of me.

"How's Lilly?" Bree changed the subject abruptly. Nonnie and Asher didn't know yet about Lilly not being her mom.

"We haven't seen her yet, Bree. Mom sent us straight home from the bakery. She was pretty bent, as you can imagine. We took the long route home, so she hasn't had a chance to lay into us yet. We'll ask about Lilly when she and Dad get home," Asher replied.

"I have a lot to tell you guys, but I hear my father pulling into the garage. We're having a later dinner here since he had to work late, but I'll try to call you back after we're finished. I'm glad you're home safe."

"Wait, Bree…." Nonnie wanted to talk more.

"I'll be in touch, Non. I promise." With that, Bree hung up the phone.

CHAPTER SIXTEEN

Milton Devon, Sr. didn't much like staying indoors on summer days. He had an array of gardens that he attended to himself. He had spent the morning admiring his dahlia garden, trying to decide, as he plucked the weeds away, which were more attractive—the yellow and pink softness of the dwarf china dolls or the knee-high dazzle of the brilliant orange Gertrude Martinek. Maybe the wistful purple of the Vera Seyfang was the best. All he knew was that he was going to spend some time with his *Dahlia's* catalog this winter. They were all lovely and such fun to grow.

Elsewhere he enjoyed cultivating and varying the acidity of the soil so that he could get different colors of hydrangeas and azaleas and orchids. Coffee was a dietary staple for him and the leftover grounds did lovely things for his flowers when he scooped them around the bases.

Many of his colleagues were less happily retired because they lacked hobbies. The elder Dr. Devon was happy to give up his position to his ambitious son so that he could spend more time doing the things he liked to do, like gardening and exploring local parks and museums and attending outdoor concerts and festivals.

He was happy until the weather confined him to the indoors. Then the shadows took over. The depths of the scotch bottle invited him into its warmth. He was alone and he never felt more so until he was inside his house.

He had thought many times since Sophie's death of selling the spacious old mansion. It was too big for him. But then where would he go? And what would he do without his beloved gardens? It was a quandary and he pondered it often.

He was moving toward his study from the mudroom at the back of his house. He had shed the muddy cotton gardening gloves and washed his hands with an aromatic vegetable soap. He had traded his molded plastic shoes for bare feet. His heart was still full with the abundant August blossoms and he was humming a Frank Sinatra tune when he slapped into the kitchen for a glass of minted iced tea. Lucretia had left it there the day before after cleaning his house.

Though Dr. Devon enjoyed the gardening very much, he didn't care for cleaning or cooking at all. That had been Sophie's job. Now he left it to Lucretia. She cleaned his house twice a week and prepared and refrigerated enough meals to see him through to her next visit. Her sister Carlotta did a fine job for Dev and both bachelors were grateful for their talents.

He took his tea and approached the dark-paneled study with reservation. There were bills that needed to be seen to. Otherwise he would avoid this room. There were too many memories and angry words exchanged in this room to spend much time here. The darkness loomed most in his study and the amber-filled snifter in the corner fairly screamed for him to dive in.

Today, though, standing in the doorway he sensed a lightening. He smelled a faint trace of lavender. He didn't see her at all, but he heard her quite clearly.

"Hello, Milt."

"Gracious, Girl. You scared me. Are you trying to give this old man a heart attack?" Milt clutched at his chest, feigning panic.

"Your heart is stronger than an ox, Milt. I just didn't want anyone else to notice that I was here. I let myself in the back while you were out admiring your flowers. They are beautiful, by the way. I had forgotten how well the moisture and sunshine greened up the gardens here. I live in the land of sage brush now, remember?"

"Lillian. You were born here. I don't know how you found it so easy to leave this all behind."

"I did it for Shannon, Milt. I did it for Beatrice. She had a wonderful, peaceful childhood. I never wanted her to know about St. Louis. Just she and I, Milt, against the world—it was always enough."

"You didn't ever want Shannon to see her again? That seems awfully selfish and final."

"Beatrice is only eighteen. She needed to get her start in the world, to know herself a little better before I thrust her complicated beginnings on her."

"So you did intend to tell her the truth someday?"

"Of course. I wouldn't have denied Shannon the right to know her daughter. I couldn't risk Dev knowing where she was, either. It's done now, though. I should have known Bree would be more resourceful than I gave her credit for. I never even suspected what she was up to."

"It's good to see that you are safe. I'm not sure why you came here, though. I can't risk having Dev know that I have been helping you. He's dangerous, Lillian. Even more so now that he has Beatrice."

"I know. I just need one more favor from you, Milt.

I need you to get me in at the hospital. You still have connections. Call whomever you have to. They are going to need a new nurse on the long-term care wing. You must see to it."

"Have you kept your credentials?"

"I have and they belong to Darcy White now."

"That was your mother's name."

"You remember. It was so long ago. I'm pretty sure Dev doesn't remember her. We were just teenagers when she died and he was off at Yale. I think he barely knew Shannon's name back then."

"I wouldn't remember except that I was a little sweet on her. She was in the same class as Sophie. It was those intriguing violet eyes. They reminded me of wisteria. You have eyes like that, Lillian, very much like hers."

"I didn't realize that you knew her."

"Why do you think I helped you? I had everything to lose."

"I thought you did it for Shannon."

"I did it for all of us—you, Darcy, Shannon. Mostly I helped because of precious little Beatrice. Dev couldn't be allowed to raise her after what he pulled. He *is* my son. But he is a monster, Lillian. A monster of proportions you might never realize."

"I've told you I don't want to know everything, Milt."

"No, you don't want to know. I didn't either. If he had any idea the knowledge I have of his activities, Dev would have seen to my demise years ago."

"Do you think he could do that to you?"

"I know he could, Lillian, without hesitation. He'll do the same to you. How can you possibly be safe at the hospital? He'll recognize you in an instant."

Lilly stepped out of the shadows. "I don't think so, Milt."

She had changed dramatically in the sixteen years since he'd seen her. Her hair was dyed dishwater blond and her violet eyes were now an unnatural green. Lilly had spent the last week in California, hiring a special effects artist to transform her. Her cheeks were fuller and she wore a fat suit under her clothing. Even if Dev were to see her, he wouldn't look twice. He admired pretty, thin blondes. He disdained fat people.

Milt himself tried to hide his dismay. She had really let herself go, the poor thing. Lillian had always been so petite, wiry even. This woman in front of him was pathetic. He wouldn't have recognized her, had it not been for the voice he was familiar with.

Lillian was slightly amused at his discomfort. If Milt was convinced, then the disguise would work. Her plan could be successful.

Milt cleared his throat. "Yes, then, Lillian. I shall make a few calls. The nursing supervisor cared for Sophie herself when she was ill. She is a personal friend now. I'm sure she can find a place for you.

"How shall I contact you once the arrangements are made?"

"I only just arrived in town. I will be making living arrangements in the next week. How about if I contact you after that period of time? You can let your friend know that I will be available to start at the end of next week."

"Very well. Lillian, you must be careful. Beatrice would be devastated to lose you. She is angry with you right now, but she loves you very much."

"She has every right to be angry. I've deceived her. But

it would be horrible to lose her to Dev and his web of lies. I will take care of everything, Milt. You will see. Get me that job. I will see to the rest."

"Good luck."

"I'm hoping I won't need any luck. Thanks, Milt."

Lillian smiled slightly and gripped Milton Devon, Sr. by his upper arms. Her eyes were reassuring. Why, then, did he feel like a goose had just walked over his grave?

CHAPTER SEVENTEEN

It was a full week before Bree had the time to call Nonnie back. This time it wasn't her father keeping her occupied—it was Benjamin.

Benjamin, besides being a debate whiz, was also a tennis star. He led the young men's bracket at the DAC in St. Louis, so summertime was a particularly busy time for him. When he wasn't playing individual matches and tournaments, he was surrounded by tennis groupies—the other teenagers, girls or guys, who were either decent at tennis themselves or wanted to be.

It was no wonder that every time Benjamin pulled up to the house, he had a red convertible full of suntanned teenagers. Bree hadn't known until that Monday that Benjamin wasn't just a teenager hanging out and having fun with his friends. He was a talented athlete with a huge local following.

Bree was having dinner with her father and Benjamin at the Club when a tall, tanned, sandy-haired man approached them. He flashed a dashing white smile at Bree, which she returned cautiously. But then he immediately shifted his attention to Benjamin.

"Benjamin Devon. I had hoped to see you here. Sounds like that few inches you've grown this year has really given you an edge."

Benjamin blushed. "I'm doing okay this summer. It's getting easier to beat those guys that I couldn't quite keep up with last year."

"You're being too modest! There are probably only two men in St. Louis who could beat you right now and they're in the division above yours."

"Benjamin. Will you introduce your friend to your sister and I, please?" Dev Devon interrupted. He didn't recognize this young man.

"I'm sorry, Sir. I didn't realize Benjamin had a sister and I haven't met you before. I only make it to St. Louis on occasion and only to check out the tennis scene. I'm Rodney Cooper. I'm a *USTA* coach and scout." He offered a handshake to Dev.

"Dr. Dev Devon. This is my daughter, Beatrice," he replied, shaking the young man's hand. Perhaps he had been wrong about Benjamin's foray into tennis. Dev had thought it a waste of time, being a water polo and diving man himself. But Benjamin had always enjoyed racquet sports much more than water sports. If he was being scouted by the *USTA*, then, Dev realized, he must be doing well.

"Your son, Dr. Devon, is the most talented prospect we have in St. Louis. He's still young enough to play the amateur circuit for another year. Do you realize that, given the right coaching and tournaments, Benjamin here could be a professional tennis player by the time he's eighteen?"

"Well, of course I know that," Dev lied. "I'm well aware of Benjamin's talent.

"But he has talents elsewhere, too, Mr. Cooper, and we've not even discussed the possibility of his becoming a professional athlete. I'm quite sure that his intended path in life is toward the practice of medicine as mine has been and my father before me."

Bree watched her brother redden with embarrassment during his father's speech and then she saw a flash of frustration cross his face at the mention of a career in medicine. By the time her father finished, Benjamin had placed his emotions in check.

Rodney Cooper looked disappointed, but undeterred. Bree could tell that he dealt with parents like Dev Devon quite often.

"I'm sure Benjamin is quite a well-rounded young man, which is another reason he is worthy of pursuit. I'm sure you'd find most professional tennis players quite intelligent. They love the sport, but it in itself is a means to an end. None of them plays professionally forever. They all develop careers outside of the tennis court later, but with the help of their earnings."

"Benjamin will never have to worry about finances while learning his occupation, Mr. Cooper. Your arguments are falling on deaf ears, I'm afraid. Benjamin may play tennis as a hobby, but I won't consider hiring a coach to take him beyond that. Now if you would excuse us while we finish our supper?"

"Of course, Dr. Devon. I'm sorry to have interrupted your dinner." Rodney Cooper directed his attention to Benjamin.

"Benjamin, keep up the good work. It's exciting to watch you play," he excused himself politely and then joined a gorgeous, glowing brunette three tables away.

Benjamin, to Bree's amazement, said nothing to his father. He had to have been crushed by their father's behavior, but he continued to eat his dinner in silence. Bree's heart broke for her little brother. He was such a smart and talented kid, but she could tell that Dev Devon had squashed whatever spirit he had a long time ago.

Lilly had cultivated BreeAnn's spirit. She had been afraid of her father at first, as she could tell Benjamin was, but Bree really had nothing to lose. She could always leave here if she wanted to. Lilly would always make sure she made it home again, traitor or not.

She waited until dessert. She wiped her mouth on the green linen napkin, took a dainty sip of coffee, and smiled a beguiling smile toward her father. "This was delicious, Father, as always."

"I'm glad you enjoyed it, Beatrice."

She turned to her sulky brother. "Benjamin, I would love to watch you play tennis sometime. I played in high school and I could use a few pointers."

Out of the corner of her eye, Bree could see her father's frown deepen when she added, "I'd like to see if Rodney Cooper and his lovely companion would like to join us for iced tea on the veranda. I just *have* to ask her where she got her turquoise bracelet."

She turned an innocent gaze back toward her father. "If you don't want to join us, Father, you could go on home. Benjamin has his car. I don't mind riding with him since he knows his way."

Dev Devon's daughter had just dismissed him. He didn't know whether to laugh or be angry. She certainly was her father's daughter. He didn't want Benjamin being sucked in by that tennis scout, but he couldn't deny that Beatrice had a sly, devilish side of her own. She was helping her misguided brother out.

In a way, it was touching. Dev would play along, for now.

Bree had never been much of a jock. She and Nonnie had played volleyball when they were freshmen and, even in such a small school, the competition to get on the varsity squad and to win matches was so fierce that neither girl enjoyed playing. From then on, they'd just stuck to tennis in the spring.

Tennis was a more individual sport and the coach in Pateros was very laid back. It was almost more folly than work. Despite her undisciplined approach to spring sports, Bree had developed a mean two-handed backhand and a speedy, though sporadically accurate, first serve.

Benjamin was impressed by her skills as they played their first match together, but he still spanked her. His first serve had been clocked. It traveled almost one hundred and ten miles per hour! She was no match for him. But they had so much fun that she decided she would play in the young women's bracket for the rest of the summer.

Benjamin's groupies were a fun-loving bunch too. They would all sit and tell raunchy jokes in the Club spa after their matches, chasing off all the stuffy old people. They alternated eating sandwiches, hamburgers, or sushi for lunch in a few quirky, hole-in-the-wall cafés in downtown St. Louis.

Benjamin told her that they did movie nights at each other's houses every Friday. The teens were all affluent and almost every home had a doting mom and a theatre room. She could tell that he was leaving something out. There was no such place or such a mom in his big old house.

Benjamin's house was a stopping point: a place they went to pick up more clothes or some soda and chips. It was never a place where they all congregated. Nobody wanted to deal with his father. He asked too many questions, made too many assertions about their activities. They'd learned long before that none of them measured up to the expectations he had for his only son.

Bree decided that it must have been very lonely to grow up the way Benjamin had. It was no wonder he surrounded himself with so many people. Bree had been happy to have just one best friend, because her other best friend had been her mom. Home for her had always been a happy place.

This revelation made her sad for Benjamin and it made her feel guilty for leaving him all of those years.

She told him so that weekend. He was good at hiding his emotions, but Bree wasn't. She wanted him to understand that, no matter how things worked out with their father, she wanted to be Benjamin's sister and friend.

"I may not be here forever, Benjamin. I've got plans to go to the University of Washington in the fall."

"Is that where you're from? Washington?"

Bree weighed whether she could trust Benjamin with that information. She decided that she could.

"I grew up in Washington. In a little town called Pateros. It's beautiful there. It's on a river too, but it's a whole lot different from St. Louis. For one thing, it's tiny, only five hundred people. And it's surrounded by high desert. Sage brush and rocky mountains are everywhere."

Benjamin was perceptive. "You must have loved it. You sound melancholy talking about it."

"I miss Pateros, but I miss my friends and my mom more."

"Our mom is here in St. Louis."

"Oh yeah, we haven't talked about that yet. Our aunt

Lilly raised me. I thought she was my mom."

"That's awful! She didn't tell you the truth?"

"I'm having a hard time believing that too. But then how could she? She kidnapped me. That's a pretty big one to explain."

"That's true. Don't you want to meet our real mom, though, Beatrice? We haven't taken you there yet."

"Father promised me that we would go there someday. I wish she was well. It sounds like she won't even know who I am."

"Well, she's never recognized me," Benjamin shared. "Who knows? She might know you, even after all of this time."

"We'll figure that out when the time comes." Bree shrugged.

"Anyway, Benjamin, I want you to know that I've really enjoyed getting to know you these past few weeks. I've never had a brother before. And you're pretty cool, you know that?"

"Yeah, I know," Benjamin teased, but Bree could tell that he was touched.

"I want you to do me one more favor, little brother."

"What's that?"

"When Father's not around, do you think you could call me 'Bree'? It's what I'm used to and it's a lot easier to say than 'Beatrice.'"

"Brie? Why don't I just call you 'Cheesy'?"

Bree gave him a playful slap on the shoulder. This was the kind of banter she'd always been jealous of with Nonnie and Asher.

"It's short for BreeAnn, you goofball."

"What's your last name? Gouda? Meunster?"

118

"You're gonna pay for that," Bree threatened, but laughed anyway. "No. It's White. BreeAnn White."

"That would make your mom Lilly White. That's quite a misnomer."

Bree shuddered as she realized that he was right.

⁂

Dev had been standing outside Benjamin's door as he and his sister talked. They had been conspirators too often over the last week. Ever jealous and mistrustful of his son, he wanted to know what was going on.

He heard every word of Beatrice's conversation with Benjamin. He'd had a number traced to Pateros, Washington. It was those kids who had dropped her off. Now he had a name.

"Lilly White," he repeated to himself. She had wrecked his daughter. He could hear her sobbing now. She had broken poor Beatrice's heart.

And she had taken far too much from him as well. He was pretty sure Pateros, Washington had never seen the likes of him. He was going to see to it that Lilly White got the full extent of what was coming to her. He would sick the authorities on her eventually, but first he was going to make her grateful to see them, because after he was through with her, anything the police could dole out would be pitiful by comparison.

CHAPTER EIGHTEEN

There was a certain breathlessness that resulted from hearing news that you weren't prepared to hear. Bree felt the pressure in her chest, the air being sucked out of the room, when she finally got around to calling Nonnie back and learned that Lilly was gone.

Whatever happened, no matter how resentful she became of her mother's betrayal, there had always been that safety net—she could go back. She knew she could always go back to Pateros. That safety net, however, was now sliced to shreds.

There was nothing left for her in Pateros. Apparently, her mother had left without warning, leaving Penny a note of apology for leaving her in a lurch, but in exchange for her inconvenience, she was being given the bakery for a tidy sum of fifty dollars.

Penny, upon receiving the note and papers at the beginning of her early morning shift on Monday, promptly turned out the lights and ovens in the bakery and marched herself over to Lilly's house.

There was no answer at the door, though the enormous yellow Ryder truck in the driveway made no secret of the occupant's intentions. The driver was asleep in the cab and he startled awake when Penny rapped violently on his window.

"What's going on, Lady? It's only…," he paused while he consulted his dash clock, "Four o'clock in the morning!

I was just catching some sleep before hitting the road with my load here."

"My best friend and boss lives in this house. Unless she's gone AWOL or neglected to mention her plans to move to the person she works with everyday, then you are trespassing by parking this truck in her drive. I suggest you hit the road now, Mister."

"Well a couple of hired guys and I had orders to empty this place and we finished pretty late last night. If your friend lives here, I don't think she's coming back, Miss."

"Who hired you?"

"Some lawyer lady in Omak hired the other two guys. I just brought the truck when she made arrangements with my boss."

"So you don't know Lilly White?"

"Nope."

Penny had walked away confused and frustrated that Lilly hadn't communicated with her. If she was taking off under these circumstances, then she had to be in some kind of trouble.

It turned out that Lilly's lawyer couldn't say much about her situation either. It was confidential. She was following the orders of her client. Denise Reynolds congratulated her on her windfall. Penny was buying a heck of a profitable business for a song.

Stress had given her a headache. Heavy dough and baking trays took more than their usual toll on her muscles. She was tired and cranky when she dragged herself home to tell Edward the news about Lilly. It exasperated her and worried her beyond reason that Lilly had disappeared.

She worked her fingers to the bone, keeping the bakery open by herself and managing to squeeze in interviews for a new baker during breaks. Then when the kids finally arrived home a week later, she had grilled them mercilessly for information about BreeAnn, hoping to get clues.

Nonnie and Asher had spilled everything. They confessed about the kidnapping, the trip to St. Louis, about Bree meeting her father, and about Lilly being a wanted fugitive.

Penny had wanted to strangle them both, but she understood their loyalty. She had taught them to always look out for the people close to them and she believed them when they said they had been looking out for Bree *and* Lilly.

She also finally understood the foundation of the one wall that Lilly had permanently and irreversibly erected between them regarding their children. Lilly couldn't talk about Bree as a baby or a daughter because she had kidnapped the child and hidden with her in the wilds of Eastern Washington, hoping that her secret would never unravel.

This angered Penny because she had been so easily taken in to love both Lilly and BreeAnn from the beginning. She couldn't even begin to understand it and neither could Edward. They both agreed that if one of them had taken one of their children from the other and hidden him or her until adulthood, their intentions would be nothing short of murderous. It was no wonder Lilly was on the run.

Nonnie shared the disappearance with Bree when she finally called her again.

It had taken every inch of her patience for Nonnie not to call back and ream Dr. Devon for keeping her best friend from her, but she knew Bree was doing what she had to do and so she had waited. And waited. And waited. Nonnie couldn't believe it took Bree a full week to get back to her. She had showered, slept and eaten with the phone on her person, waiting for it to ring.

Bree could feel Nonnie's displeasure. It was palpable despite the miles between them. She absorbed and briefly mourned the news of her mother's disappearance. Once she caught her breath, she spent the rest of the time doing damage control. And she asked about Asher, his white smile flashing in her mind's eye as she spoke his name. Nonnie said he was working, a lot, trying to make up for leaving the Quick Stop in a lurch while he was gone. He was also helping Penny in the early morning hours after leaving his late shift.

Bree spent nearly a half hour soothing Nonnie's chafed feelings and she was about to hang up when she remembered what Nonnie and Asher didn't know about her and Lilly. She had learned the truth right after they left, but there had been so many secrets, that she hadn't realized they didn't know her relationship to Lilly.

"There's something you need to know, Non. I almost forgot to tell you, because it felt so huge when I learned of it and you had barely walked out the door. My grandfather told me that Lilly isn't really my mother."

"*WHAT*?" Nonnie couldn't take this intrigue any longer. That had to be the topper. "You were kidnapped by a stranger?"

"Not exactly. Lilly White is actually Lillian Waters and she is my maternal aunt, my real mom's sister."

"So you're saying that you have a real mom, Bree. How could you forget to tell me about that? And where is she? Why wasn't she at the mansion when we were there?"

"That's the saddest part of all of this, Non. She went nuts when Lilly took me. She's in a mental hospital and I haven't gotten to see her yet."

"You know what, Bree? Lilly White, for being practically the coolest person I ever grew up around is turning out to be the baddest of the bad. I don't get it."

"You and me both, Nonnie," Bree sighed. It was far easier not to talk about the heavy stuff because it reminded her that her time in St. Louis wasn't all fun and games. She had some serious issues to work out before the rapidly-approaching Fall and she wasn't getting any closer to the answers she needed.

"Can you tell Asher 'Hi' for me, too, Nonnie? I miss you both so much and I'll try to be better about calling, okay?

"From your mouth to your oh-so-limber dialing fingers, Bree. I love ya, kid."

"I love you too, Nonnie."

———

Lilly hadn't disappeared at all. In fact, quite the opposite was true. There wasn't a desktop or hospital bed or tray table that she didn't graze with her ample buttocks these days. She just couldn't get used to her wide load. It didn't help that it was impossible to put a nervous system into a fat suit—it was as numb as a diabetic's toenail.

She realized immediately after starting her job that she didn't miss nursing at all. The State Hospital had grown from a mental health facility to a full-blown hospital. She was put to work as a Medical-Surgical nurse with no access to the inpatient psychiatric facility, but she planned to work her way there.

The Med-Surg nurses were an apathetic lot. She discovered that many had long ago lost their desire to help people and had become *Oz* to the poor midget nurse's aides. They pretended to write care plans on the computerized charting system while checking their *E-Bay* accounts and calling to harass the overworked attending residents about medications or restraint orders.

Lilly didn't want to call attention to herself by being friendly to the aides, but she had spent too many years in customer service to let her patients languish in uncomfortable circumstances. If a commode needed emptied, she didn't push the button for the aide. She did it herself. Though the computer system was daunting, she took the time to learn it and to chart as she always had— meticulously.

She wasn't winning many friends among the other nurses who labeled her as a do-gooder, but they largely ignored her. After all, she was sort of plain and fat, not much to look at really. As long as she didn't rat them out for their laziness, they left her alone.

Lilly endured her miserable job the first two weeks, working as many shifts as she was allowed, trying to get into the good graces of her supervisor. August was turning into September and, if she knew Dev, he would be getting his hooks into Bree effectively by now. There was still Bree's scholarship at the University of Washington. School wouldn't start until the end of the month, but Lilly felt a renewed sense of urgency as the balmy air grew crisper to see her sister and blow Dev's cover.

She saw her opportunity on a quiet afternoon. They were overstaffed. Three of their patients had gone home that day and Lilly volunteered to leave early. She went by the nursing supervisor's office on her way out.

"Good afternoon, Ms. Wolley," she greeted the amiable woman with the full white bun and loose-fitting, bohemian clothing. Virginia Wolley looked up from a half-completed schedule on her laptop as Lilly walked in.

She greeted 'Darcy' warmly, dropping her violet-rimmed reading glasses to the end of her nose. This woman had become a nursing director by sheer hard work and experience. These new nurses coming out of school frustrated her to no end with their desire to earn a paycheck and perform minimal dirty work. Virginia Wolley had been a nurse when a nurse took pride in good work done, in showing up a doctor or two, and in providing ultimate comfort for the people in her care.

Virginia remained seated and invited Darcy to sit down. She'd known right away that her new charge was cut from the same cloth and experience as she. Darcy White was 'old-school' and that made her special in Virginia's eyes.

"Are you enjoying your work here, Ms. White?" Virginia closed her laptop softly and moved it to the side.

"I am. I haven't thanked you for hiring me on Dr. Devon's recommendation. It was a risk and I appreciate it."

"Don't mention it, dear. Milt and I go way back and he hasn't called in many favors over the years. What do you think of our Med-Surg unit? I noticed that most of your experience was psychiatric, but the opening was on the general floor."

"Well," Lilly chose her words carefully, "It is different in a lot of ways from psych nursing, but I'm getting the hang of it."

"I sense hesitation. To be quite candid, I've had

nothing but trouble keeping that unit staffed. Good RN's are just so hard to find anymore."

"I wasn't going to say anything about that, Ms. Wolley. I'm just so grateful…"

"Say no more, Ms. White. Since you're here, though, we have been given notice by one of my oldest and best nurses on the long-term psych floor. She's finally decided to hang her hat, lucky woman! I have a month to fill the position, but I was wondering if you might be interested. You are certainly qualified."

Lilly quickly did the math. A full month would be a long time to wait, but it was probably her best opportunity thus far.

"I would love to apply for the position," she replied enthusiastically.

"You needn't apply, dear. If you want it, it's yours. You'll just simply transfer departments. It'll be nice to see you at work in the area you love. You're a shining star among nurses, Ms. White. Hold your head high and don't forget it."

"Thank you so much, Ms. Wolley," Lilly flushed a little at the unexpected compliment. Maybe she hadn't lost her touch after all.

"Call me Virginia, Darcy. Everybody does, whether I want to allow it or not! I want you to start training with MaryJane on the long-term ward next week, if that suits you. That way you'll be able to suitably replace her when she goes."

Next week! That was perfect. She was on her way.

"That will be wonderful," Lilly shook Virginia's hand. 'I'm coming home to you, Shannon,' she thought, returning Virginia's warm smile as she began to plot her next move.

CHAPTER NINETEEN

The girl had spotted him and was reaching for him, pleading with her eyes that he should help her, stop the monster from taking her air and her life away. Her lips were rimmed in gray. She struggled and flailed her hands in the air, never taking her eyes from his until they bulged unnaturally and became void and her body fell limp.

Those haunted eyes stayed in his mind as Milton Devon, Sr. startled awake in the early light of a late August Sunday. It seemed he couldn't clear his vision of those blue eyes, even as he fumbled with the bedside lamp. He was perspiring, feeling panicked as he always was when he had this dream.

He called it a dream, a recurrent nightmare. That the dream had its roots established from his traitorous memory further terrified him as he awoke from its ugly grip. Her eyes had been so clear, so blue, so young, not even a line marring the fine skin around them.

Milt knew who had killed her. He'd seen it happen and he had stayed hidden, shame and fear conquering his instinct to help her. What had happened to him? He had once taken an oath to care for people to the lengths of his ability. He was a doctor. He wondered when he'd lost his ability to distinguish the power to heal from the knowledge that he could get away with just about anything, using that power.

There was a snifter of brandy on his bureau. He often

resorted to a slip of it when he couldn't find sleep for fear of allowing the memories back into his psyche. He took comfort in that bottle now. The nerves needed calming. It was too early to go out to the garden and too late to go back to sleep, so he would do his best to soothe his conscious self.

When his breathing returned to normal and his heart was no longer threatening to jump out of his chest, Milt sat upon his green leather bedroom settee with his half-filled glass, allowed himself to think back over the dream, and his mind shifted back to that horrible day sixteen long years before.

He had been in Dev's office at the hospital. Being chief of staff had allowed him keys to all of the offices of the medical staff and he had needed to talk to Dev about Sophie's medication. Her tolerance to it was increasing and he had needed Dev to make corrections in her prescriptions. He would have done it himself, but it was widely understood that it was inadvisable to treat one's own spouse.

Milt had been waiting on the camel-skinned davenport when he heard a young woman's voice, sounding shrill and slightly hysterical just outside the office door. Dev had been evasive as of late, not allowing Milt and Sophie to visit him at home. He said it was because Shannon was so ill after her second pregnancy, unstable really and she wasn't in any shape to have guests.

Milt could hear Dev raise his voice just slightly, demanding that the young lady step into his office in order to avoid a scene. Milt, out of natural curiosity, hid himself between the walnut-paneled wall and the black-lacquer bookcase, parallel with the door. Dev wouldn't notice him there unless he sat behind his desk and put on the overhead light. Milt gambled that he would do neither. Dev disdained fluorescent lighting and almost never lit more than his green pool lamp while he worked at his desk.

The girl, for that's what she was, really, was red-faced, calling Dev innumerable colorful names as he shoved her through the door and closed it behind them.

He whirled on her, looking embarrassed, more furious than Milt had seen him in quite some time.

"What, in God's name, do you think you're doing here? Why aren't you at the house? What makes you think that you can come to my place of work and make trouble for me?"

"Divorce her, Dev. I'm tired of waiting for you to take matters into your own hands. You'll listen to me, now, *Dr. Devon*, if you don't want me singing to the hallways and the heavens about what you've done."

"You should know better than to threaten me, Diana. You've reaped plenty of benefits in exchange for your trouble. I will never divorce, Shannon. Think how that would look. Part of being a prominent and admired physician is being seen as a dedicated family man as well. My father taught me that. The home must never be disrupted, especially not for a whiny opportunist such as yourself."

"That's a laugh, Dev. You, the family man—it's an illusion, a lie and I'm going to expose the truth."

"Why? So that *you* can be the woman of my house? That would never happen. You're simply too young. You lack poise, polish, sophistication. My wife needs those qualities."

Dev took a cigar from his desktop humidor and rolled

it thoughtfully between his delicate hands.

"I was good enough for you to bed, though, many, many times?" She leveled a seductive gaze at him.

"Yes, of course. You pursued me, Diana. Remember? I simply took what you offered." Dev lit the cigar, puffing and winking suggestively.

This further infuriated the girl, who coughed and waved away the acrid smoke.

"So all of the times you slid your hand up my skirt and eyed my chest, even before I offered anything else, was that all my fault, too? You'll give me more, or I'll tell everyone what you've been up to, how you harassed me. I'll even tell your father."

"You're going to have to do better than that. I'm not afraid of my father."

"I'll take your son away from you."

It was the ultimate threat, for he had lost his sweet little girl just a month before. She, too, had been taken. He'd be damned before that would happen again. He would find Beatrice and nobody would even be allowed to take Benjamin.

Milt watched as the thin string of patience that Dev had displayed visibly snapped. He suddenly stabbed out his cigar in his marble ashtray, and rose from the edge of the desk where he'd been perched. He walked the few feet to the defiant girl and backhanded her violently across her right cheek.

She burst into tears, holding her bruised face.

"You won't get away with this, Dev," she cried quietly, pleading. "You can't beat me and keep me quiet. I love you and you love my body. Divorce her."

"I will never divorce Shannon."

"Divorce her," she repeated, louder, sobbing.
"Never."

Then Dev did something Milt never imagined he was capable of doing. He grabbed the girl about the throat and shoved her backwards onto the davenport, straddling her with his knees. He kissed her violently. Tears were sliding down her cheeks, but she was unable to talk. Then Milt's son set about strangling this young girl. She spotted Milt, during the struggle, to her left and kept her gaze directed at him, begging him silently for help, her eyes bulging and then becoming blank as her life blinked out. Dev was apparently so caught up in the act that he never even looked Milt's way. Dev stayed there, straddling her body, until his breath returned. Then he returned calmly to his feet.

Milt stayed frozen while Dev hid the body in his bathroom, pausing to brush his teeth and comb his disheveled hair. He straightened his tie and brushed his white lab coat free of the signs of a struggle. Then he calmly replaced the partially smoked cigar in the top drawer of his desk, wiped his face of its horror one last time, took a deep breath and went back to work.

As soon as the door closed, Milt checked the girl briefly to make sure that she really was beyond help. Then he sat with his head in his hands for an interminable amount of time, contemplating what to do. Finally deciding to do nothing, for he hadn't the courage, he exited the office about fifteen minutes after Dev. His son didn't, indeed, fear him, but Milt was plenty afraid of Dev, especially now.

He buried the memories as deep as they would go. He denied himself any acknowledgement of his son's activities. But those dreams, they would never let him rest. He could never erase those. Alcohol and death would be his only escape. On mornings such as this, the latter couldn't come soon enough.

CHAPTER TWENTY

BreeAnn finally worked up the courage to talk to her father about college the first week of September. She and Benjamin had been spending most of their days at the club, meeting their father for dinner in the evenings. Dev had returned to his normal, hectic work schedule and he actually felt some relief that Beatrice had something useful to occupy her time. Tennis was good exercise and he could be sure that no one would be recruiting her for her efforts.

Those pesky scouts had continued to bother Benjamin and Dev held firm in his resolve that Benjamin should finish high school and move on to a university, without a thought to a career in tennis. It was rubbish and he wouldn't hear otherwise.

Still, it secretly pleased him that his son was so admired. Now his daughter, too, attracted attention at the club with her newfound confidence and sophistication. She'd learned to dress correctly and to curtail the shyness and hesitation that had accompanied their first weeks together. She and Benjamin were becoming good friends, and conspirators. Their laughter and sparkle as they shared daily events with their father filtered out into the rest of the room and Dev knew he was envied for his gorgeous family.

It was as it always should have been.

He knew, too, that he and Beatrice needed to talk about college. She shouldn't be allowed to languish here. He was sure that she would have had college plans in Washington.

His investigators had learned that she was at the top of her class in Pateros. She was bright, of course, despite her wily aunt.

It frustrated Dev to the point of hysteria that no one had been able to track down Lillian Waters. His investigators had trailed her as far as California. She had disappeared exactly three days after Beatrice's arrival and she was, no doubt, on the run from him. Well it was wise for her to be afraid really. But she would eventually be caught. He had the best agency money could buy on his payroll now.

He shrugged off thoughts of Lillian. It was useless to fuel that anger now—better to save it and nurture it for when he could actually torture her with the knowledge that she had not won Beatrice after all.

His reverie was interrupted by his daughter.

"Father. Father?"

Bree wondered where his mind had wandered this time. Her father was a thinker above all else and sometimes he retreated rather unexpectedly. It was not a good place he was in right now. He looked strained, vaguely angry.

"Yes, Beatrice. I'm sorry, dear. I'm afraid I've worked so much lately that I've become rather tired. Forgive me for wandering off."

"Don't worry about it, Father. You do work too hard."

"It takes dedication, Beatrice, not just to become a doctor, but to be admired and revered for years in the practice. I've been meaning to discuss this with you, Beatrice. Your education is critical to your career if you're planning a career in medicine. I'd be happy to talk with you about it, if you're interested. Many young women are studying medicine now.

"You could follow in the steps of your grandfather and I," Dev finished, convinced that his daughter would find this a viable career path.

"I have thought about medicine, Father. Even before I knew about you and Grandpa, I'd thought that might be what I'd study. You know what's interesting? I thought about becoming a Psychology major," Bree laughed at the irony of that given her obvious family history of mental illness.

"Don't you dare, young lady. Psychology would make you a counselor or a therapist, an underling in the world of mental illness. If you want to deal with mental health, you'd best be looking at a medical degree. Any child of mine will take the most educated approach, to be sure."

Benjamin interrupted, "You already have plans for going to school this fall. You should tell Dad."

To his father, he added, "She's got all kinds of scholarships and she's been accepted to one of the best schools in Washington State."

Bree reddened. She shot Benjamin a look. They'd discussed whether she would talk to their father about college, but she'd been waiting to see what he had in mind before she made any admissions or decisions.

Benjamin blanched as he realized he'd told his father too much. Bree was really shy that way. She was intensely private about her life before, which he understood because she was protecting her Aunt Lilly, but he couldn't let her get by without standing up to their father. He'd cowed to Dev's ideas and opinions all of his life, but seeing his determined sister over the last few weeks had fortified him. She needed to tell him about the University.

"Beatrice, would you like to tell me what your plans

136

were for the fall quarter, before you came to St. Louis, that is?"

Dev presented an open front, wanting her to tell him as much as she would about her life before. He'd stopped pretending that there was no life in between her babyhood and now. He genuinely wanted to know about his daughter and what he had missed.

"I have enough scholarships to completely pay for my attendance at the University of Washington this year. I was admitted to their Biology program originally, though I'm not sure I'll stay that path. I was waiting until I got there to see how I would like it."

"Why, that's wonderful, Beatrice. You are a smart girl, aren't you, to have earned your way into such a prestigious school? Why in the world would you feel you needed to keep this from me?" Dev feigned hurt.

"You're only just getting to know me again. I didn't want to tell you right away that I was planning on leaving at the end of September. To be truthful, I was afraid you'd make me stay."

"I must admit that I don't want you to leave at all, Beatrice. You're right. I'm selfish and I don't want to let you go far away again, but if it's what you want, then so be it. Promise me one thing, though."

"What's that?" Bree was apprehensive.

"You must let me call an old friend of mine who's a dean at Washington University here in St. Louis. He may be able to see if there's a place for you here. It's a wonderful research school and you could stay closer if you were accepted."

Bree felt a pang as she realized that her future as she had planned it might just be in jeopardy. Her father's heart was in the right place, but she hated to change plans so that she was further away from home—her real home. It meant further distancing herself from Nonnie and Asher, and, if she ever made a reappearance, Lilly. Staying here would also be giving more control over to her father. She wasn't sure she trusted him enough.

"So you'll let me check into it, Beatrice?" Her father interrupted her thoughts, seeing in her clear moss eyes that she was troubled.

"I suppose that would be okay."

"That's my girl. You'll love it if you stay. I'd be overjoyed if you stayed. And I'm sure Benjamin, here, would love to keep his big sister around."

Benjamin knew Bree had just given license to their father's hopes for her. He hoped she was ready for the ride, because it was going to get bumpy.

⁓

It was later that night and Bree was washing her face in her adjoining bathroom. She heard a light knock on her outer bedroom door. Dabbing her face dry, she glided to the door, thinking Benjamin might be coming by for a heart-to-heart.

But it was their father at the door. She was surprised, because ordinarily when they left the club, he held sanctuary in his bedroom suite before they all went to bed. It wasn't that he was antisocial, he just preferred to unwind in his favorite place in the house. Bree had rarely seen him in his pajamas, as he was now, all navy-blue silk and white monogramming and piping.

She bit back a smile. Her father never stopped dressing in his finest, even when he donned his pajamas.

"Father. I thought you'd gone to bed."

"I will soon, Beatrice. There was something else I wanted to talk to you about tonight and I didn't bring it up at dinner, because I didn't want to upset Benjamin."

"What is it?" Bree opened her door wider, inviting her father in where he could talk to her without Benjamin overhearing.

Bree perched herself on her pink gingham chaise while Dev remained standing. This room was so 'girly.' It made him enormously uncomfortable, so he cut to the chase.

"I've made arrangements for you to meet your mother tomorrow."

Bree had been hoping for such a visit for so long that she'd almost given up hope that her father would arrange it. She was at once nervous and excited. She was going to meet her biological mother, Lilly's sister. She wondered if she would see a resemblance.

"I'll look forward to it. What time do I need to be ready?" Bree maintained her cool. Dev wouldn't want her overly excited. He could deem it as distressing to her mother.

"I'll come by after office hours and pick you up at about four. You mustn't get your hopes up about Shannon, Beatrice. She's been ill for a very long time. The chances that she'll recognize you are very small. Still, I promised that you would get the chance and she's been medically stable for a while now, so I see no need to delay any further."

"I'll be ready. I have a question, though. Why would it upset Benjamin that I'm going to see our mother?"

"Well, I haven't taken him in a while. It upsets him to no end that she won't recognize him. He just doesn't understand why he can't awake some feeling or reaction from her. I didn't want him to go again only to be disappointed. Nor did I want him to be jealous should Shannon have some recollection of you."

"I understand. Thank you for arranging this, Father. It's something I need to do."

"I know, Beatrice. This meeting is inevitable. I just wish there was some way I could make it easier for you."

"You don't always need to make things easy for me, Father. I can handle this."

"That's my girl."

There was that possessiveness again. She gave him a tentative hug anyway.

"Good night, Father."

"Good night, Beatrice. Sweet dreams."

Chapter Twenty-One

Lilly spent her first days as a long-term nurse meeting and greeting all of her 'charges.' It was a large unit, housing as many as thirty patients at a time. The nursing staff was large and competent—they were dedicated to each and every patient and his or her comfort.

What warmed Lilly the most was that despite the terrible mental debilitation some patients displayed, the underlying current of hope in this wing was palpable. It never occurred to this staff that one of these patients might never be well again. They'd all seen miracles and they'd seen suffering at its most acute. Their job was to prevent the latter and hope for the former.

It fortified Lilly that nobody had given up on her sister. She hadn't either.

Their reunion was anticlimactic, really. Lilly had pretended not to know the famous Dr. Dev Devon's tragic wife, Shannon. She had greeted her just like the others, with warmth and cordiality. Shannon had stared into space, her left hand laid over a tablet of paper next to her, absently flipping the ends of the pages.

She still appeared strong, though she was heavier than Lilly remembered, probably because her mobility was limited by her catatonic state. She was still able to walk, though, and was allowed into common spaces with other residents, but Lilly learned that Shannon mostly preferred to stay in her room.

Her visage was sad, tragic. She looked as if the world had been at the tip of her fingers and someone cruel had yanked it away. Her spun-honey hair was graying at the temples and flowed in thick waves to her shoulders. She wore a yellow, calico-print flannel gown and fuzzy pink slippers. Some of the residents were given to dressing for the day. Shannon never did. She preferred her pajamas and the staff demurred to her preferences.

The only thing that hadn't changed about Shannon was the deep lavender of her still young-looking eyes. They were unspeakably sad eyes, but Lilly could see, as she looked into them that they still had the soul of ages. Shannon was the younger of the two of them, but their parents had always claimed that she was an 'old soul.' She was wiser and more cautious and, in so many ways, more pensive than Lillian had ever been.

It was no wonder that she had been the one to end up perpetually despondent. Lillian didn't believe, though, that she was catatonic because she was mentally ill. She knew that the responsibility for that rested solely with her dear husband, Dev Devon.

What she wasn't positive about, though, was whether Shannon's state was from a breakdown that occurred after Lillian and Beatrice left, or if, as she suspected, Dev was medicating her into being this way. If he was drugging her, it wasn't apparent in her medical chart. The medications appeared standard—vitamins to prevent communicable infections, anti-psychotic drugs to keep her from harming herself or any other patient, anti-depressants to elevate her mood—all of these were standard and the doses looked correct as well.

Any peer reviewing Shannon's chart would admire Dr.

Devon's obvious painstaking attention to his wife and her care. It wasn't usually ethical for a spouse to be assigned to his own wife's care, but Dev had insisted out of guilt and devotion that he, and he alone should be allowed to care for Shannon. Peer quality review, for this reason, had been frequent. His colleagues had been impressed with her treatment and progress.

Dev even visited Shannon frequently, at least twice a week. His visits were kept private. The staff understood his need to have time with his wife. It had been like this for nearly seventeen years. The nurse that Lilly was replacing had seen the entire drama unfold. She, like the rest of the staff, was touched by Dr. Devon's continuing loyalty to his wife.

Lilly was fully aware that Dev Devon was revered here. She was unfazed by it. She didn't trust him. She assumed that his intent was far more malicious than anyone would dare suspect. Her sister was not this ill on her own. She would prove it. She was going to ruin Dev Devon, for Beatrice, for Shannon, for all of the years they had all lost.

It was Thursday, the first week of September when Lilly overheard the other day nurses gossiping. It seemed that Shannon's long-lost daughter had shown up in St. Louis in August. They hadn't seen her yet, but rumor had it that Dr. Devon was planning on bringing her that very day.

They were abuzz. Who would the girl look like? Would she elicit some response from her poor mother? Would they bring that good-looking Dev miniature with them again? He seemed so upset every time he left, poor thing.

Lilly was so keen to lay her eyes on Bree that it nearly

pained her to anticipate it. She was well disguised. She knew her daughter would never recognize her unless they were to talk face to face. After all, she'd given Shannon some very pointed eye contact over the last week and she hadn't seen any spark of recognition.

But there had been a moment, just that morning, when Lilly had leaned in close to her ear and whispered, "Oh, Shanny-dear, I do wish we could talk like we used to."

She'd used the endearing term their mother always used for her. Lillian had been 'Lolly-girl' and Shannon had been 'Shanny-dear.' Lilly could almost hear her mother's Irish lilt in her own voice when she had whispered to her younger sister.

Lilly had pulled back from her sister then and seen the most miraculous smile pulling at the corner of her little sister's mouth. Her eyes registered one sweet moment of joy and then they grew blank again.

It lifted Lilly's heart and then laid it bare again. Her sister was in there and she would reach her, somehow.

Lilly would keep her eye on Bree and Dev, but she knew she'd have to keep a safe distance, or Bree would recognize her voice instantly.

They arrived at five o'clock, having come from an early dinner in the cafeteria. Dev had worked his office hours and arranged for Carlotta to drop Beatrice off to meet him in the hospital atrium. They'd talked quietly about what Beatrice should expect from her mother. She should say what she needed to, but as calmly as possible, so as not to upset Shannon's delicate state.

They didn't generally touch Shannon, because it usually made her flee. Any physical contact would usually result in a few days of complete antisocial activity from

144

her—it was as if she was afraid to be touched again.

Bree was prepared for all of this, but nothing prepared her for the lovely violet eyes that stared from her mother's face. Their hair was somewhat different because Shannon's was grayer and she appeared heavier, perhaps taller in build than Lilly, but those eyes, deeper purple and the exact same shape as Lilly's, took her heart and flipped it right over.

Her eyes were indescribably melancholy, with none of the happy sparkle that often spilled from Lilly's. But, oh, they had to be sisters. This was her mother. While Dev hovered in the doorway, Beatrice rushed to her mother and knelt before her. She gazed imploringly into her mother's face and she spoke softly.

"Mommy? It's me, Beatrice."

Dev was pierced through the heart with the tenderness of the moment. This should have happened so long ago. If only Shannon's sister hadn't interfered, he might have made them all a family again. He had taken care of the one person who threatened to tear them apart and he had searched mightily, yet in vain, for his daughter for all of these years, just so that they could all be together again— he, his wife, his daughter, and his son.

Was it too late? Shannon had withdrawn further and further into her illness. He wasn't sure if it was an actual breakdown, or if the injectable drug he'd given her twice weekly, away from prying eyes, had taken her reasonability away entirely. *Risperidone* was for schizophrenics, which Shannon was not, but it had done a fantastic job of keeping her medically restrained and it was long-acting.

He wasn't sure, but now seeing his wife and his daughter together made him think that he might be able to back off the dosage a little and see if she would improve.

145

The only problem was how he would brainwash her, should he allow this to happen. She had threatened once, years ago, after Beatrice disappeared, that she would sing to the heavens that Benjamin wasn't hers and that Dev was keeping her prisoner. Chances were that she might not even remember these facts this many years later, but he'd had to silence her then and he didn't want to do that again.

He loved Shannon. He always had. Even when she'd forced him to look elsewhere to satisfy his body's urges, he'd still held her in the highest regard. When they'd first been married, they'd been happy companions, delighting in their house and their travels. And when their daughter arrived, they doted on her together. They were superb friends, even when she turned him away for a short time as a lover.

He'd puzzled over how he would regain his beloved Shannon for years. Beatrice's arrival made this an even more perplexing problem. Could he erase only the bad memories from Shannon's brain? Could he gradually let her out of her personal hell and then insert his own version of the truth into therapy sessions?

When his daughter's soft plea evoked a tear from Shannon's eye and prompted her to reach out and stroke Beatrice's white-blond hair, Dev knew that he must try. The syringe he had in his pocket would languish there. He'd wondered how he would give Shannon her medicine with Beatrice there. Well, he wasn't going to give it to her, this time.

⸻

Lilly really and truly despised Dev Devon. She always had. Trying to look involved in her charting, she nonetheless looked up once in a while to shoot daggers into his back as he stood in the doorway of her sister's room.

She knew that he'd loved Shannon, giving her everything—a home, travel, lovely things—when they were married. But he'd also possessed her sister and he'd taken her health away from her because he'd produced an illegitimate child with a girl that was younger than Bree was now.

Lilly wondered where that boy and his mother were now. He had Beatrice back. She wondered about Shannon's fate, now that she'd seen her daughter again. Dev Devon held all of the cards. Well Lilly was going to see how to shuffle that deck. Seeing him again had reinforced her hate of the man. While she'd yearned to go to Bree and give her comfort as she faced the difficult task of reuniting with her mother, Lilly had swallowed the idea and added it as fuel to the fire that was going to burn Dev Devon alive.

CHAPTER TWENTY-TWO

Bree returned home exhausted, spent from the emotional toll of seeing her mother so sick and unreachable. She'd looked so much like Lilly. She'd known instantly how much she'd lost by not knowing her all of these years. Her mother had obviously lost even more.

She was silent in the car all the way home. Her father's mind had taken its leave again. He had nothing to say that could comfort her, so he said nothing and retreated to his own thoughts of trying to heal Shannon.

Upon arriving at the house, she went immediately upstairs, threw herself on her bed, and called Nonnie on her new cordless telephone extension.

It was only noon in Washington, but she hoped Nonnie would be home anyway. She wasn't sure if Penny had gotten more help yet or if Nonnie would be at the bakery. Lunchtime was extra busy at the River Run. At least it always had been. She really missed the bakery. She missed just everything.

The phone rang four times and, finally, a groggy deep voice answered.

"Hello?" Asher's voice sounded like sugar, the deep timber instantly warming Bree's wounded heart.

"Hi Asher. It's Bree."

"Bree? Oh my Gosh, Bree. How *are* you? Is Dr. Devon treating you right? You sound upset."

"You sound sleepy. Did I wake you up?"

"Yeah, but that's okay. I've been working until three and then helping Mom with the early morning baking. I get home at about eight every morning. She's really busting my chops! She's been doing some interviews, though, so it looks like there's an end in sight."

"That's good. I'm sure my mom, um, Lilly, misses being there with her. I'm worried about her, Asher."

"We are all worried, Bree. It's probably best that she left, though. Did you know that your father has people prowling around, asking questions about her?"

Bree was alarmed. She hadn't known that her father knew Lilly's location. How could he have found Pateros? Were his intentions malicious? If they were, Lilly was probably in real danger of being arrested, or worse.

"I didn't know he'd tracked her location down. You know, in a way, I'm as angry as can be at Lilly, but I still don't want her hurt. I met my mother today, Asher."

"What was she like? Nonnie said she's in the hospital."

"She's very sick, Asher. She recognized me, though. She couldn't speak to me, but she felt my hair and she cried. She looked so much like Lilly, but a little different. Her eyes were the same."

"Does she have those cool purple eyes like Lilly?" Asher was intrigued.

"She does. In a way, she looks way too young to be my mom. She doesn't have any wrinkles. But she has these gray streaks at the sides of her hair that betray her age. She's beautiful, really, but tragic," Bree shivered involuntarily as she remembered how quickly her mother's eyes had gone blank after she began to cry.

"Are you doing okay?" Asher was her hero, still. It was so comforting to have his voice so near, so soothing.

"I'll be okay, Asher. I just needed to talk to you or Nonnie. Benjamin is cool, just a cute kid, but he hasn't ever gotten our mom to recognize him, so I knew I couldn't talk to him about this."

"Are you going to come home, Bree? Nonnie and I are leaving in a few weeks. I've already started to pack for the few hours in the evening that I'm home and awake. I'm going to Cheney September twenty-third."

Bree yearned to tell him that she would come home before then. They were supposed to all be together in the days before they went their separate ways. At least then they would have the opportunity to ponder missing each other. As it was, she felt like she'd already lost them. Their last precious times together had been sucked into her complicated lost life.

"I don't know, Asher. I want to come home. I don't just miss Lilly. I miss everything: the fresh, baked bread, the nighttime chill of the river air, the walk to the quick stop with Nonnie to harass you during your night shift."

Asher smiled. He was going to miss all of that too when he left.

"My father is seeing if he can get me into Washington University here in St. Louis. He's told me that I can go to UW if I want to…."

"But he wants to keep you in St. Louis," Asher finished for her. Dr. Devon was going to do his best to control Bree, he knew, with his money and his influence.

"It wouldn't be so terrible. Homesick as I am, I'm going to be leaving anyway. This way I could be closer to my brother, too. I could also go visit my mom again."

Bree was trying to convince Asher that her father's intentions were good. He didn't buy it.

"You have a tough decision to make, Bree and I won't make it any harder for you. Just remember how hard you worked to get to UW in the first place. It was all you, Bree, all your hard work and persistence and your smarts. Nobody pulled any strings to get you there. That's something to be proud of."

Asher had never told her he was proud of her before. It warmed her and made her miss him more. It also fortified her when her emotions had been laid flat. He was right. She had worked hard. But that didn't make it any easier to defy the hold that her father had taken on the rest of her life.

"Thanks, Asher. I needed to hear that. I'm really beat, though. I'm going to take a nap before dinner. You probably need some more sleep too."

"Sleep is overrated. I'll tell Nonnie you called. She's helping Mom with the lunch crowd, but she'll be home before too long."

"It was good to hear your voice."

"Yours too, Bree. Be good and be careful."

"Bye, Asher."

Bree replaced the cordless in the charger and laid her head back down on her pillow. In an instant, she was asleep.

⸻

Back in his study, Dev stopped the recording device he had on Beatrice's phone. He was frustrated. It sounded like the people back in Washington still didn't know Lillian's whereabouts. He'd been listening to Beatrice's calls to glean this information, not to invade her privacy. At least that's what he told himself.

But that sly, young Native American fellow was trying

to weasel Beatrice into leaving him again. It was okay, because he could outfox just about anybody. He just needed to lay on the charm with Beatrice. He also needed to give her mother back to her. There was no way she would leave if her mother needed her. He knew that's what she yearned for, to have a mother figure back in her life.

He would do his level best to see that Shannon got healthy again, through careful medication and counseling. In the meantime, he would devote a little less attention to catching Lillian. While he was keen for revenge, he knew now that Beatrice was onto him on that front.

He carefully hid the wiretap recorder behind the heavy doors of the walnut armoire and walked quietly up the stairs to his sanctuary. He paused as he passed Beatrice's door. She was silent, obviously taking the nap she had admitted to needing.

Benjamin was still at the club and dinner wouldn't be served for another few hours, so Dev decided to rest a while himself. For the first time ever, his bedroom suite felt empty and lonely. He realized that the physical satisfaction he'd taken behind these walls, discreet as it was, was no substitute for the feelings he and Shannon had generated here so long ago.

She had decorated this place and she had brought the warmth and familiarity to it in the first place. Now that he'd resolved to help her, the suite would never feel the same until she returned. Dev was unable to sleep, so he resigned himself to watching mundane television in his recliner until his mind stopped churning and committed itself to slumber.

Chapter Twenty-Three

Milton Devon, Sr. rarely visited St. Louis State Hospital. It had once been the center of his career and his life. His wife, Sophie, had often joked that she needed to arrange an apartment at the hospital so that she would see him as much as his nurses and patients did. Now, though, he didn't care to frequent its hallways.

For one thing, it had been thoroughly remodeled and added onto since his time there. It was a veritable maze and Milt was overwhelmed by the consuming changes. It had been simply a psychiatric facility when he started there. Now it was a full-blown, state-of-the-art hospital.

For another, the memories of this workplace were all too acute. He'd been here, working, when Sophie had birthed their son across town. He'd been just a resident then and he hadn't been able to get away and see his wife and son for a full forty-eight hours.

He'd gone on to become a chief resident, then an esteemed medical staff member. By the time he retired, he'd been the chief of staff and his son had been well on his way to following in his father's footsteps.

They were opening a new outpatient rehabilitation wing and had offered to name it for he and Sophie in honor of the sacrifices they'd made out of dedication to the hospital. He wasn't sure he was worthy of such an honor.

Painful memories always burbled to the surface when he came here: The time that Sophie had come to confront him with rumors that he'd been misusing hospital funds, padding his pockets, so to speak.

It had been true. He'd seen the opportunity to allign a few of the hospital's deposit accounts to his own bank account. He called it his 'recruitment fund.' If a few luncheons and rounds of golf were had from this fund, it was only for the good of the hospital. That it had also bought a brand new, baby blue, BMW convertible was only because he needed to arrive at work in style, an example of all that could be achieved by hard work and dedication.

Nobody had been hurt by the small amount of pilfering until Sophie had found out what he'd done. She'd been irreversibly disappointed by it. Then she told Dev. Dev saw to it that the accounts were reassigned and that his father's embezzlement went undiscovered by the board. He had protected his father.

Then Dev had caught him in a most compromising position with his nurse, Helga. She'd been bold and beautiful and German and Sophie had cut him off at the knees with the whole money business. He had needs, as any man did. When Helga had offered herself to him, blond and sinewy and laid out on his broad mahogany desk, he'd taken her. He'd been pumping his heart out when Dev walked in the door.

His son's expression had been stricken, full of hate for this man that he'd once admired wholeheartedly. Milt often wondered if Dev would have been such a calculating, cold menace had he not been so thoroughly disappointed by his father. His son had closed the door immediately and Milt had wilted with shame.

Milt had atoned for his sins with Sophie, never being unfaithful to her again, and never leaving her side when she was diagnosed with a brain tumor. Her mental status had been affected mightily by her inoperable disease. She'd acted as if she despised him by the time she died. Dev had undoubtedly hated him, though obligation kept him from cutting Milt off completely.

Sophie had died two years after Milt watched Dev kill a young woman with his bare hands. There was no longer any threat of his beloved wife knowing the extent of his indiscretions, but Milt never could bring himself to confront Dev with the crime he had committed. Perhaps it was guilt, perhaps shame, perhaps loyalty that protected Dev.

Milt didn't know. All he knew was that he truly hated this place. He came once a month to see Shannon. Like Lillian, he suspected that her illness was Dev's doing. His silence had cost her as well. So he spent time with her the second Tuesday of every month, like clockwork. It was the day Dev designated for staff inservices, so his son was scarce and Milt had time to really examine and evaluate Shannon's condition.

What he couldn't figure out was which drug Dev was using to limit Shannon's mobility and speech. The charted medicines didn't have this effect on the level of awareness she displayed. He'd seen the evidence of needle sticks on the back of her left arm. No one else was apparently aware of these.

Milt was standing in the doorway, the second Tuesday of September, wondering if Shannon had finally gotten a visit from her daughter, when he noticed something different about Shannon. She had glanced at him, looked him over properly, and then returned to her inner thoughts. He was stricken. She hadn't looked at him, really looked at him, in years.

This was progress. He was elated and cautious. Perhaps his son had just not had time to dose her yet. He was about to enter the room to see if he could get her attention again when a fat nurse with faded blond hair and unnatural green eyes touched his elbow and gestured to the opposite hallway. It had taken him a moment to realize that this was Lillian. She'd made her way back to her sister's floor, the clever woman.

"Milt. How are you? I didn't know you came to visit Shannon."

"Once a month, dear. I tell myself that I'm coming to see how she's faring, but I do find myself evaluating her at the same time. You can't take the hospital out of the doctor, can you?"

"No. Not in your case," Lilly cut to the chase because she didn't want to be caught ignoring her other duties.

"Something is happening with her, Milt. She's started looking at people. She still retreats into that silent world of hers, but the eye contact is different."

"Perhaps that son of mine has stopped undermining her care."

"You'd better be quieter with those accusations, Milt. He can't know that we're onto him. She started improving the day that he brought Beatrice."

"Maybe that is what made the difference," Milt supposed.

"Maybe. But I don't think so. She's been more active, too, taking walks around the common areas. I didn't see her do that for the first week and a half I was here."

"I have a suggestion, but it will take some finesse to pull it off, er, Darcy.

156

"What's that?" Lilly knew this wise old doctor could help her get through to her sister.

"Her oral medications include anti-depressants and anti-psychotics. The anti-psychotics are making her less energetic, less aware so that she won't act out. The anti-depressants are keeping her mood elevated and keeping the anti-psychotics from making her sleep overly much. Do you usually give her the required medications?"

"I am responsible for all morning medications, charting and dispensing to this half of the floor. I don't provide the evening dosages, though."

"Is there anyway that you can make the morning dose disappear for those two medications?"

"Would they kill the plant on her nightstand?"

"I guess you will have to find out. Just be careful. It won't do your sister any good if you get fired. You'll have to be sly."

"What if she does come around, Milt?"

"Scary, isn't it? We won't know the turn her emotions will take once that happens, but you'll have to wait and see."

"I have to go back to work before someone gets curious as to why I'm talking to you. That kind of stuff will inevitably get back to Dev," Lillian shrugged and walked back to the front common room to recover a lap blanket for a young man absently watching game shows on television.

He watched her walk away. It really was tragic that she'd let herself go so. She'd been a striking young woman at one time.

Milt returned to Shannon's doorway, crossed to her side, and whispered her a hello. Then he tried to look deep into her eyes. For a moment he was sure she looked back.

Though he often avoided touching her, because he knew it disturbed her senses, he took a chance and squeezed both of her forearms.

"Shannon, darling, you really do need to come back to us. You're probably the only one who can set all of this straight for Beatrice. Fight for it, please. Lillian and I, we will take care of you."

Milt saw a glimmer of familiarity flash in Shannon's eyes at the mention of her sister.

"Oh, yes, honey, she's here and she's taking care of you, just as she took wonderful care of your daughter. Beatrice has turned out to be a gem. You can be proud.

"Now fight, Shannon. For Beatrice. For all of us."

Milton let her arms go and she crossed and rubbed them absently, then she nodded almost imperceptibly.

It was just four days later, with her psychiatric medications discontinued, that Lilly popped by on her day off, with the excuse of retrieving a sweatshirt that she'd left. Her colleagues had noticed that she favored a few of her patients, which they all did. Shannon Devon was one of these and it wasn't entirely unusual for one of them to visit a patient even on an off day.

Lilly was there at medication time and the nurse on duty was about to give Shannon her cup of pills. They'd all noticed small changes in Mrs. Devon and it generated some excitement. 'Darcy' feigned concern about their patient's progress. Abigail, the other registered nurse, had met Darcy White on her first week at SLSH. She was a good one. Abigail wondered if Darcy might finish giving this patient her pills while she moved on. She was short an RN and she had twenty-eight other patients to see to on the morning rounds.

Darcy was happy to help. She took the cup of pills and went to the sink to fill a Dixie cup with water. If a few of the pills accidentally washed down with the water, it wasn't apparent to anyone but her.

She took Shannon her vitamins and the glass of water.

"Here you go, Shanny-dear. This should be a little lighter than usual."

Shannon took the cups in both her hands and looked Lilly right in the eyes as she swallowed both of the vitamins down.

Her voice was wasted because she hadn't used it in so long. It came out in a faint croak, but the words were unmistakable.

"How sister get in there?"

"Oh, Shan. It is me in here. How'd you know?"

"Voice."

"Milt is right. I am going to take care of you."

Shannon's eyes teared up, as did Lilly's. They'd both lost so much. Reuniting was going to take years. All of the words would come out eventually. For now, though, they had to be cautious.

"Shan, you have to be so careful. Dev is still here a lot. I don't know why, but he's stopped giving you the medicine that takes you away from us."

"Shots." Shannon had known what was happening to her.

"If he knows I've taken away the other medications as well, he might start giving you the shots again."

"Help me, Lillian."

"You can help, Shannon. You need to be silent when

159

he is here. Try to avoid looking at him. He'll notice that you've improved, but he mustn't know how much. He doesn't know that I'm here, either. If he did, I'm sure he'd kill me with his bare hands. He knows I've had Beatrice all of these years."

"Beatrice."

"Yes, she's gorgeous, isn't she? I've been so sick that I couldn't share her life with you, Shannon. I couldn't have any contact with you because I didn't want to take a chance that we'd be found. She's smart, that one. She found her own way back to her father. That's why she's here. I'd hoped she'd never fall into his clutches again."

"Don't let hurt her."

"I will die before I'll let him hurt her, Shannon. You know what he's done, don't you?"

"Remember a lot."

"He can't know this, Shannon. Whatever you do, don't ever let on that you remember.

"I have to go, Shan. It would look odd if I spent any more time with you on my day off. I'm not sure I can get back tomorrow without seeming suspicious. So I need you to do one thing for yourself. You need to avoid swallowing the green and the red pill in the cup they give you. They are both small and they might take you away again. We need to get you well, Shannon, and get you out of here, away from Dev."

"Already know. Didn't take pills last night. Put in plant."

"Good girl. That's exactly where I'd put them! Keep going, Shan. You're going to get your life back. I promise."

Lillian stole a quick hug for the first time, reveling in the softness of Shannon's hair. It had been so long since

160

she'd held her little sister. They were going to get a lot more of these moments if she could pull this off. She pulled away and stole out of the room, visiting her other 'favorite' patients before she left, so that she'd appear to be paying attention to someone besides Mrs. Devon.

She went into the fresh September Saturday air with renewed vigor and sense of hope. Life was good, better than it had been in a very long time.

Chapter Twenty-Four

Dev had no problem getting Beatrice into Washington University. His friend, the Dean of the Pre-Medicine department, Manfred Gibbons, had been happy to do Dev a favor. Dev had taken care of his daughter when she'd attempted suicide as a teenager and she'd come out okay, thanks to careful medication and counseling. Dr. Gibbons and his wife owed Dev far more than a favor.

Dev scheduled a dinner at *The Painted Duck*, a hip downtown brewery/restaurant, in celebration of Beatrice's acceptance. He didn't tell his children why they were celebrating, but asked them both to dress for an occasion.

Beatrice looked clean and scrubbed, her blond hair pulled on top of her head. She was dressed tastefully in a black pencil skirt and a simple emerald shell blouse. She was stunning, without realizing it. Benjamin had been at the club all day and had gone home to dress afterward. He was dashing in a black suit and silver tie. Together, they were a picture and he was so proud of the both of them.

He waited until dessert to make his announcement. He gave each child sparkling cider to match his own champagne. Beatrice was intrigued. Her father was elated, in a splendid mood. What could they be celebrating?

Dev held up his glass. "Here is to my lovely daughter, Beatrice. Honey, I am so proud of you and I know you've worked so hard to get into college and to succeed beyond your current level of education. I am delighted to help you with this. That's why I'm so thrilled to tell you that your hard work has resulted in another acceptance into a university.

"A colleague of mine, Dr. Manfred Gibbons, has seen your transcript and your test scores. He was delighted to accept you on behalf of Washington University into the Pre-Medicine program. Congratulations, Beatrice. You've been accepted into one of the most prestigious universities in the Mid-West. Let's give a toast to your success."

"Here. Here," Benjamin responded appropriately. He had been hoping Beatrice would stay. This was her chance.

Beatrice's reaction wasn't quite so enthusiastic. She lowered her glass and asked quietly if she could please speak to her father in the car. She didn't want to cause a public scene because that, above all else, would annoy her father. Dev was displeased, but he complied, leaving Benjamin with his pocketbook so he could take care of the bill.

Beatrice and her father walked quickly to the car, which the valet had brought around in record time. The concierge could see trouble brewing and he'd been on the ball.

"You'd better start explaining this behavior right away, young lady."

"Stop, Father. I waited until we got to the car because I didn't want to disappoint you in front of Benjamin and everybody else in the restaurant. I'm not going to stay here in St. Louis. I want to go back to Washington State for college. I hadn't made my decision even as of yesterday, but I know now that's what I want to do. I love Seattle and I don't want to change my plans."

"What about your brother and your mother. You know

she recognized you, don't you? How are you supposed to reach out to her again if you leave? What about me, Beatrice? We are only just getting to know each other," Dev was pleading with his daughter.

She remained reticent and calm. It was time to ask her father some questions.

"I need to know something," she asked quietly belying the turmoil she was actually feeling.

"What's that, Beatrice?"

"How did you know which high school to get my transcripts and test scores from? I never told you where I was from."

Dev was taken aback. He'd never been asked to explain himself by one of his children.

"I'm resourceful, Beatrice. It has taken me far. You've talked about your hometown within my house, haven't you?"

"You've been listening to my conversations? With Benjamin or on the phone?"

"Both, Beatrice. You didn't really expect me to accept your word that you'd had a happy childhood without finding out if this was true? I was looking out for you, darling."

"Don't give me that! You were snooping! You wanted to find out where I was from so that you could hurt Lilly, my mother, or the woman I always thought was my mother."

"That's not true."

"Well, even if it's not, she's gone. You can't hurt her."

"I'm angry with Lilly and she should pay for what she did, taking you away from Shannon and from me. But I wouldn't hurt her. I would only let the authorities take the

164

proper action."

"She must have had her reasons, Father. I've been meaning to ask you: Do you know what those reasons were?"

Dev was nonplussed. Who was this defiant girl? He didn't like being interrogated. She needed to show some respect.

"There would never be enough reasons in the world to take a child away from her parents. It was selfishness on Lillian's part, pure and simple. She didn't have a child of her own and she took you. She broke my heart and your mother's fragile health. I don't ever want to hear you question me again. I am your father and you will show me more respect than this if you expect to stay in my household.

"Furthermore, I got you this chance at the University so that you could remain close by. I thought it was in your best interests."

"You don't know what my interests are, Father. You don't have to worry about me respecting you, because I don't need to stay in your household so that you can spy on me further," Bree moved to get out of the car.

Dev grabbed her forearm. "Beatrice, please. Where will you go?"

"I'll find my way home. I could stay with Grandfather for now until I could find a way back to Washington."

"You can't do that. He's an unstable old man, Beatrice. I won't go into details, but I don't think it would be a good idea for a young girl to stay alone in his household."

"What are you implying? That Grandfather is a pervert?"

"I just don't think that he'll be helpful to your cause,

Beatrice. I'm sure he's as interested in keeping you here as I am. Please, just come home with Benjamin and I. I'll give you your privacy, I promise. I just want you to spend some time really considering what I am offering."

"I haven't heard any apologies, Father. How am I supposed to trust you now?"

"I am sorry, Beatrice, for having invaded your privacy. Please know that I was only trying to protect you."

"I don't believe you."

But Bree knew that she was cornered.

"I will go home with you, for now," she capitulated reluctantly.

By this time, Benjamin was waiting on the sidewalk, his hands jammed into the pockets of his trousers. He looked impatient, and concerned.

"Should we let your poor, suffering brother into the car, Beatrice?"

"Come on, Benjamin. Get in," Bree couldn't help but smile back when her brother flashed her a charming grin.

"Can I ride shotgun, Sis?"

"You're a pain in the rear, Benjamin. Pull the seat forward, will you?" Bree poked him in the ribcage and climbed into the back seat.

"We've got her for now, Benjamin," Dev feigned a conspiratorial demeanor. "Should we take her home or do we find some other kind of torturous method of keeping her here in our town?"

Bree didn't feel like playing along. This night had been trying already. "Can we just go home, guys?"

They complied, both feeling dejected, lost in pondering how to keep her with them.

Bree hadn't slept well with thoughts warring in her head about whether to stay or to go. She was furious with her father for invading her privacy, but without his help, she wasn't sure really how she would get home or where she would go in the meantime.

She finally stopped fighting for sleep when five o'clock ticked past on her bedside alarm clock. She dressed quietly and went directly to the foyer hall tree, where Benjamin unfailingly hung his car keys. He was his father's son, despite himself, because he was just as organized and predictable. It made stealing his car easy.

She was going to the hospital to see her mother. It was way before visiting hours, and it was a Sunday, but she would find a way to finesse herself into her mother's unit. After all, she was Dr. Dev Devon's daughter.

Beatrice had memorized the way on their silent ride home just the week before. She drove the few miles quickly, given that there was no traffic this time of morning.

Just a short while later, she was looking at the door to her mother's room.

The night shift was still on duty and the nurse insisted that Mrs. Devon would still be asleep, but he conceded that Bree might wait for her in the bedside chair as long as she promised not to actually wake the patient.

She didn't, either. She watched her beautiful mother sleep peacefully and she saw her open her remarkable violet eyes when the sun pierced the curtains at precisely six thirty. She looked surprised to see Bree. But to Bree's utter amazement, Shannon nonetheless recognized her and reached for her.

"Hi Mommy. It's Beatrice again."

"You don't need to tell me. I know."

Bree stared on in complete awe. Her mother was talking! It was a miracle. No wonder she'd been so eager to see her mother. Some part of her must have known that Shannon would come around.

"You sound wonderful, Mother! I'm so happy that you know me and want to talk to me. It's all I've dreamed about since I learned that you were alive."

"Missed you, Beatrice."

"I'm sorry I was gone so long. I was taken away and I didn't have any control."

"Know. Just a baby. Wanted you to have Lillian."

Bree wasn't sure she'd understood the last part correctly.

"You wanted Lillian to take me? Is that what you're saying?"

"Yes. Wanted. Didn't trust your father. Told Lillian to take you."

The earth whirled a little faster on its axis for a few moments in time as Bree took in the knowledge that her mother had authorized her kidnapping. Lillian had only acted on her sister's wishes. That changed everything. But the mystery still hadn't completely unraveled.

"Why didn't you trust my father?"

"Long story. Drugged me. Cheated. Lied."

Bree didn't trust her father either, but she hadn't expected that his transgressions included drugging and torturing her mother.

"Must go with Lillian again."

"I can't, Mother. She's gone. I called home to my friends and she has disappeared. I'm not sure where I can turn for help to get home again and try to find her."

"Lillian's here."

168

"She's *here*? How could she be here? My father will find her. It's definitely not safe for her here."

"Disguised, Beatrice."

"How am I going to find her, Mother? I found out last night that my father has been spying on me so that he could learn Lilly's whereabouts. He's trying to keep me here with him and, though I'm glad to be with you, I want to go back home for college. I don't know how I'll get home without his support."

"Lillian's fat, now. Green eyes, too bright. She's nurse. Milt. He will help find her."

Then Bree saw Shannon's face grow ashen as she saw Dev pass by through the viewing window. She was terrified of her husband. Bree was starting to feel that way too. He saw Bree at the bedside and rushed into the room. Before she knew it, her mother's face registered nothing of the light it had when she'd been talking to Bree. Shannon had tuned back out for her husband's benefit.

Bree saw him tense. He was angry with Bree for coming here without consulting him. Shannon had been showing visible signs of improvement, according to the staff, but he didn't want to upset her into a setback.

He wanted Beatrice to spend time with Shannon, but only under the right conditions. He had to make sure that Shannon wouldn't recollect her ordeal before he let his daughter spend unchecked time with her.

He greeted Shannon warmly and ordered Beatrice quietly to go home. It was far too early for her to visit his patient. Bree complied. She was going home, but only after she'd gotten some answers from her grandfather, Dr. Milton Devon, Sr.. It was a good thing it was Sunday, because Benjamin wouldn't be getting his car back anytime soon.

CHAPTER TWENTY-FIVE

The air was getting crisper each and every day as September progressed. Milt wasn't much of a church-goer, so on Sunday his sanctuary was his garden. He was tending to his plants, pinching off the spent blossoms, putting peat moss lovingly around the bases of the plants that would need additional blanketing as the weather turned colder.

The leaves hadn't yet started to change color, but Milt knew they would soon. Fall for him was like mourning, because he knew the winter to be most confining. Winters were not terribly harsh here, mostly rainy, but they could be bitterly cold and oppressive, forcing Milt indoors where he dearly hated to be for an extended length of time.

So he was spending as much time as he could in the gardens now, while the weather was good. They'd had a pleasantly dry month and his flowers had required more watering, but he found the work pleasurable.

His granddaughter found him in his garden, humming the tune to "My Girl." He had a lovely baritone. She hadn't known her grandfather was a singer. There were many things mysterious about this old man. She'd only seen him a few times, just once here at his home, and he hadn't shared much about himself. Beatrice had seen pictures of Sophie and asked about her. She could tell it pained him that she was gone.

Milt Devon had always seemed odd, a bit eccentric, but gentle and kind and he seemed to genuinely care about

Beatrice's welfare. She was going to have to trust him now, if her mother was to be believed.

He hadn't noticed her yet and she could nearly tap him on the shoulder. Not wanting to startle him, she instead cleared her throat loudly as a clue to her presence.

He startled anyway. After all, he didn't take many visitors, hadn't for years.

"Oh, Beatrice. I wasn't expecting you, child."

"I didn't know I was coming until a short time ago, otherwise I would have called."

"You don't need to call ahead, dear. You are always welcome here. It's a joy to see you."

"I'm afraid, Grandpa, that my visit isn't going to be pleasant for you. I have questions, so many of them and I'm beginning to be afraid that my father won't want me to know the answers."

She continued, "He loves me, but I'm beginning to feel like being loved by him means being controlled by him as well. He wants to control where I'm educated, what I study, when I visit my mother, who I talk to on the phone, what I wear. It bothers me and it scares me because I'm starting to feel like I can't trust him."

"Feelings like that can often be relied upon, Beatrice. My son does have control issues. That I'll concede to. You're right, though, that he loves you."

"My mother is afraid of him."

Milt raised his eyebrows. He hadn't visited Shannon since Lillian had planned to change her medications. If Beatrice was sensing real changes in her mother, it meant Dev would also.

"How do you know this, child? Shannon hasn't spoken to anyone in years."

"I don't know why, Grandpa, but she's talking again. Do you know what she told me today? She said that she didn't trust my father. She said that he'd drugged her and cheated on her, lied to her and that she'd told Lilly to take me away from him."

By now the two of them had made their way to the veranda. Milt all but fell into the whitewashed cast iron chair.

"Please sit down, Beatrice. You must, because I don't think we can have this conversation standing up."

Milt removed a red bandanna from his back pocket and wiped the sweat from his brow. He didn't know where to begin sorting the truth from the lies with Beatrice. He wasn't sure he knew all of the truths himself.

"First of all, I must say that I'm very concerned for Shannon that she's communicating these things. Because if she is, that means Dev will find out. I don't know what price he'll pay for her silence, but he's paid it all of these years. If he's letting her out of her shell, he's going to do it cautiously. She can't be put in jeopardy like that again."

"I'm not sure how, Grandpa, but she must know this, because her awareness vanished as soon as she knew Father was watching her. She didn't let on that we'd been talking at all."

"When did all of this happen?"

"Earlier this morning. I haven't had much sleep, trying to sort everything out. Until this morning, I was angry with my father for interfering in my life. What teenager doesn't feel that way? After talking to my mother, I'm terrified that he's capable of inflicting real damage. Grandpa?" She looked imploringly into his ocean blue eyes.

"I know what you're going to ask me, Beatrice. He's

my son. You want to know what he's done and what he's capable of doing." Milt looked mournful, but he was determined to help his granddaughter now, as he had many years before. Her safety was foremost and she wasn't safe with Dev any longer if he suspected her defiance and fear of him.

"I need to tell you what your father's done, Beatrice. I love him because he's my son and he will love you forever because you're his daughter. But this family has some bitter, dark secrets and it's time you knew them all.

"Dev's desire to control the people he loves has taken years away from your beautiful mother. I could never let that be your fate. I'm going to tell you everything, but I'm going to start with myself. Come into the house, Beatrice. We will have some mint tea."

Milt set the table with shortbread cookies and tall glasses of minted iced tea. Bree noticed the discomfort with which he moved about the kitchen. It was clear that he didn't spend much time here. It took him three tries to find the cabinet with the cookies. He also couldn't figure out the ice dispenser built into the refrigerator, so he resorted to fishing the cubes out of the icemaker inside the freezer door.

She waited anxiously, not wanting to betray her impatience. She was here for answers, not a late morning snack. She could tell her grandfather needed the fortification and, as if her body betrayed her curious mind, her stomach growled at first sight of the biscuits.

Milt settled himself into the bistro chair opposite Beatrice. He took a long sip of tea, then he settled one fine-boned hand upon the other on the tabletop and he began to speak.

Bree almost wanted to cover her ears and turn away from the acute shame her grandfather displayed as he told of his own abuse of power, of conceit and infidelity. It was almost more guilt than one man could bear, especially since his son was privy to all of it.

Those transgressions, though, had nothing on the tale of her grandfather watching her father kill a young woman, even younger than Beatrice, with his own hands. It was almost too gruesome to be true, and she was inexplicably mortified that her grandfather hadn't been compelled to turn his son in, sins be damned.

Instead, he'd allowed her father to cover up his crime however he saw fit. He'd aided Lillian as she stole away with Beatrice. He'd buried his wife with the full extent of his secrets safe, yet he'd still kept his silence. Her grandfather had known for nearly seventeen years that her father was drugging her mother to keep her locked in a mental institution, unable to share what she knew about him.

Bree hated him for keeping these secrets, but she admired him for telling her despite the obvious pain it cost him.

Beatrice wanted to know what her mother knew that had endangered her father so. Milt explained what he suspected, but was never sure of—that Benjamin was not Shannon's son at all, but the son of the young woman Dev had strangled. The only piece of evidence being that the girl had threatened to take him away. It had been one of the last things she had said before she died.

The timing of Benjamin's birth had also coincided with Shannon's sudden irreversible illness. It also explained why Benjamin had never awakened any emotions from

Shannon's psyche. There was no emotional attachment, no recognition of a baby boy she did not bear.

They'd finished their tea and cookies and Bree felt as if she'd watched a horror movie where one character after the other had opened the one door that she knew hid the greatest danger. She felt embattled. It was all too surreal, her family's past. Until a few months ago, she hadn't known this family existed. Now she knew too much. Was she to accept the sins of her grandfather and her father, and go on living with the knowledge that the suffocating love shown to her was at the cost of lies too enormous to bury?

Milt watched Beatrice, waiting for the hate to register. She'd once had a loving, doting mother and a close circle of friends, a promising future, and a childhood filled with innocence and fun. Now she was thrust into a family with more deceit than true caring. It hadn't been her choice, really. She'd just wanted to know the truth, not to be devastated by it.

Bree had been so traumatized by the events of the last couple of months, that she'd started to check emotions at every door. Instead of reeling with this news and running crying to another room, she was like a veteran doctor staring at a gruesome trauma scene. She was already calmly dissecting the situation and taking stock of her options.

"I can't stay here, Grandpa. I think you know that."

"Yes," was all Milt could reply.

"I can't return to my father's house because I'd never be able to look him in the eyes without acknowledging that he was capable of killing someone. I'd be terrified."

"That's understandable."

"I don't want to stay with you, either. You've told me the truth and I appreciate that very much, but I wouldn't be

175

comfortable staying here when my father would be able to look here for me."

"This would be one of the first places he'd look, Beatrice."

"I realize that. My mother said you could help me find Lilly and that she's here in St. Louis. Could I possibly stay with her?"

"I would certainly be able to connect the two of you, but I'm afraid that I can't put Lillian in that kind of danger. She's safely able to roam the halls of the hospital and take care of your mother. Short of keeping you locked up in her apartment, what would she do with you while she tried to avoid discovery herself? She's doing remarkable things to aid your mother's recovery. She must be allowed to do this until we can bring Shannon to safety."

"You're saying that my presence would just complicate things. So you must have some other solution, Grandpa. Tell me what I need to do."

"You need to go home, Beatrice. To Washington. To your friends and your university. Go on with your plans."

"I don't even have a home to go back to. Lilly has had it emptied and put up for sale."

"Then you must stay with your friends. Don't go back to Dev's home, Beatrice. Your safe escape means no more contact with your father, at least for now. I will purchase your plane ticket and bus fare. I will also give you money for clothing and expenses, because I'm sure you will need to shop for new things to replace the things you'll have to leave behind."

For a moment, Bree flashed to the closet full of new, designer clothes at her father's house. She mourned it, briefly. It was just clothing. It could all be replaced.

176

"When will I leave?"

"This afternoon or tonight—as soon as possible, Beatrice."

"What if my father's investigators are still prowling the town of Pateros?"

"They could alert him as to your whereabouts, but they could never force you to go with them. You are an adult now."

"He could show up there himself and demand that I come back with him."

"Beatrice, you're going to have to trust Lillian and myself more than we've proven we can be trusted. We are going to bring Dev to justice. We have no physical evidence against him, so we're simply going to have to force him to reckon with his mistakes, however we have to. He won't have time to come after you. If Shannon is doing as well as you say, he will have his hands full."

<hr/>

BreeAnn was on a plane to Seattle before nightfall. It was a blessedly direct flight, which meant that she got to spend her time crossing half the country with her exhausted eyes closed. The next flight left a half hour later, taking her to Wenatchee, where she was enveloped immediately inside the terminal by the arms of Edward, Asher, and Nonnie.

She hugged Nonnie and Edward first, then Asher gave her a chaste hug, pulled back and gave her a searing, grateful look. With that look, he leaned forward, gently cradled her face in his hands, and gave her a lingering warm kiss. He tasted of hot cinnamon gum and sunshine and his soft black hair brushed her forehead as he pulled away. She got a glimpse of impossibly white teeth as he smiled in retreat. She couldn't help but smile back.

Nonnie looked on in astonishment. Her brother and Bree had been holding out on her. Her reaction as Asher leaned over to grab one of Bree's bags, was to pinch his upper arm, hard and twist. Her eyes said they would talk about this later. Bree simply blushed and followed them out into crisp late summer evening.

They'd insisted on meeting her plane. She hadn't wanted to trouble them. They wouldn't have had it any other way. They'd been waiting for six weeks to see her home again. It seemed like a lifetime to Bree. She knew as they chatted the entire way home that she'd been mistaken to think that her real life would be anywhere else but here. St. Louis was an illusion, a dangerous web of lies and she'd been caught up in it.

It was euphoric to drive back into Pateros. She would only be here for a week before she'd be leaving again for Seattle, but she took comfort in being here for now.

The Pakootas' household hadn't changed a bit. She and Nonnie talked into the night. Bree told her everything and her friend held her tight as she cried. Bree was safe and the ground was stable beneath her feet.

All would have been right with the world on the next sunny Eastern Washington morning, except that now both of her moms were missing. They were still tangled in that web and Bree was anxious to know how they would escape unscathed.

CHAPTER TWENTY-SIX

Milt returned Benjamin's car the day that Beatrice left, leaving the keys with Carlotta, and walking the short distance home.

Thus, it was easy for Dev to deduce where his daughter had gone. He called his father first, Sunday evening, inquiring as to his daughter's well being. He asked that she be put on the phone so that he could explain why he'd been so short when he'd found her with Shannon.

Milt wanted to buy Beatrice as much time as possible to return home securely. He refused Dev's request to talk to his daughter, claiming that she didn't really care to talk to him. He suggested, in his most fatherly manner, that his son should give her modicum of space to sort out her feelings about her mother and father. She was an adult, after all.

Dev was incensed, but after thinking it over, he could see his father's reasoning. Beatrice just needed time to cool off. She was safe at his father's house, despite the insinuations he had made otherwise. He would give her a day or two and then she would come back to him. Surely she would see that he had her best interests at heart.

Dev waited until Tuesday evening before he showed up at his father's doorstep. Milt was quite surprised that it had taken that long. Dev wasn't known for his patience. Milt answered the door nonchalantly.

"Why, Dev, I wasn't expecting you. You could have called before coming over. I would have dressed."

Milt was still wearing his filthy gardening clothes and his house slippers. He was carrying his dinner plate with him and moved to set it on the marble foyer table.

"Cut the crap, Father. Are you eating by yourself? I would expect you to take better care with my daughter here. I realize that you've been alone for quite some time, but have you lost track of your manners entirely?"

Dev's disdain for his father's bachelor habits had been no secret between them. Living alone was no excuse for letting one's self languish.

Dev let himself in. Milt made no move to stop him. They stood there in the evening silence, sizing each other up. It was Dev who finally spoke first.

"Are you going to tell me where she is? I really need to speak to her, to make her understand."

"What is it that she's to understand?"

"That I am looking out for her and that I want to keep her close to her brother, her mother, and me. I was wrong to be angry with her. I am asking her to give up everything she's ever known. I know that, but it is for the best."

"I think we should talk in my study," Milt gestured to the back of the house. Dev followed, reluctantly. He knew his father was seeking his bottle of scotch. It meant Dev wasn't going to like what he was about to hear.

Milt lit the desk lamps and poured them both a finger of scotch. Dev had never had much of a taste for it, but he took a sip anyway.

"She's not here, Dev."

"What do you mean 'she's not here'? Where did she go? Is she out with Benjamin? I haven't been home since work, so I haven't seen him tonight."

"She's left. I've sent her home to Washington State."

"You've *what*?" Dev was furious. This so undermined all of his plans. It took every ounce of self-control not to fly over the desktop and shake some sense into his father.

"She couldn't stay with you after knowing the truth. I've told her everything."

"You've made a grave mistake, Father. You know that I have the power to make your life miserable, don't you? I'm sure the hospital wouldn't mind inspecting the accounting from all of those years ago. Are you sure you'd be able to pay them back?

"They'd also be interested to know that one of their most esteemed colleagues was a philanderer. I'd bet they wouldn't name that new wing after you and mother after they learned of your tryst with Helga, in your office, no less."

"You know, Son, I've feared your threats for so long. I've finally realized why: It's because I'm a coward. It's just that it's too late now to feel shame and regret. I've felt them for so long that they're no longer relevant. The only person who would have really cared is gone. Your mother never knew about Helga and I never betrayed her again. She's gone, so it doesn't really matter now."

"You're wrong about that, Father," Dev knew how he could hurt his father most and it was time to strike out. "I told Mother everything. She and I had no secrets. You see, we *trusted* each other. I would never have kept anything that significant from her, even though it hurt her terribly."

Milt closed his eyes and he nodded. It made perfect sense. He'd always believed, hoped, really, that Sophie's brain tumor had poisoned her mind against him. Milt hadn't believed his son callous enough to ruin their bond completely.

"Then there's nothing left to hide, is there, Son? She really was the world to me. I'm sorry you had to destroy her opinion of me. I never would have done the same to you in her eyes."

"What could I have done to cause my mother any pain, Father? My life has been nothing short of tragic. She was sympathetic. You never showed me the same kind of support."

"That's because I knew what you'd done," Milt was exasperated that his son should still feign innocence, play the victim after all of these years.

"Dev, you murdered a woman in cold blood in your own office. You drugged your wife for nearly seventeen years and had her committed. You led your son to believe that his own mother didn't recognize or care about him, when she wouldn't have, would she?"

Dev's face paled and he drew himself further into his chair. He'd thought Shannon was the only one in the world who could ruin him. He'd had no idea that his father held even more secrets than his wife. They were the only two people in the world who knew about his connection with Diana. This meant only one thing—he would have to decimate his father. He couldn't be allowed to spread this filth.

"So you told Beatrice these lies, also, Father?"

Milt simply nodded.

"Well it's no wonder she left. You have no proof of any of this, do you? How could you convict me in the eyes of my child without evidence to back up your claims?"

"Dev, you know that I have no proof. I wonder why, then, Beatrice believed me. She must have already had reason to mistrust you."

"Well if you're going to reveal my evil secrets to everyone, you might as well know them all."

"What else could there possibly be, Dev?"

"Don't you think you should be asking me *why* I've done these things? It's not my fault that I'm dysfunctional. I grew up with a father who spent almost every waking moment from my birth forward involved in his work. I idolized you anyway and I sought to be like you. Then I found out how little nobility your life really contained. You were a shameful embezzler. Then shortly after that, I found out you were a cheat as well.

"I never could get that picture out of my mind, you know, of you laboring over Helga's half-naked body, sprawled across your desk. Why do you think I felt compelled to try the very same thing with Diana? She offered herself to me and I recreated that scene, many times, in my own office."

Milt felt the bile rise in his throat. His son truly did hate him.

"It wasn't my fault she became pregnant, but when she did I couldn't just turn my back on my child. She told me after it was far too late to take care of things. She'd also known it was a boy. I wanted my son. I wanted Shannon to want my son. It was only after she wouldn't comply that I decided there had to be a medical way to make her agree.

"If Beatrice hadn't disappeared, I believe I could have made her well enough again to understand and to accept Benjamin as her own child. If Diana hadn't gotten so pushy, I could have let her be involved with our son as well. Nothing happened according to my plan, Father. I never intended for anyone to get hurt."

"But they did get hurt. Did you tell your mother all of

183

your secrets as well, Dev?"

"You leave Mother out of this. I didn't need to tell her. She was too ill by then. She couldn't have handled the strain."

"So much for your wonderful, *trusting* relationship," Milt sounded as bitter as he felt.

"You don't get to talk about my relationship with my mother. I loved her completely and she loved me. It was the only uncomplicated relationship I've ever had. You betrayed her even up to the very end."

"I didn't, Son, I swear," Milt defended himself. "I took care of her, even when she hated me."

"But you wouldn't do the one last thing that she asked of you. She was suffering so the last few months of her illness. The headaches were excruciating."

"I did my best to control her pain. I had you adjust her medications when it seemed necessary."

"She wanted you to help her die, Father."

"I couldn't do that, Son. It wasn't ethical. Besides, I couldn't bear to watch her die at my hands."

"It was what she wanted—the last thing she wanted from you after you'd destroyed every ounce of admiration she ever had for you."

Milt began to cry, to mourn yet again for his beautiful Sophie. She'd always been the light of his life. It just about killed him that he'd disappointed her so. His courage had waned at the most crucial times.

"I couldn't kill your mother, Dev."

"I did it for her, you coward. I got to see her luminous eyes say goodbye as she went peacefully to sleep. I let her die under her terms. You had failed her, again."

Milt's voice was weak as he faced the wretched

184

monster his son had become, "You killed your mother, too?"

"I let her die with dignity, something you couldn't let her do."

"Get out of my house."

"You can't get rid of me that easily. I will never let you spill your lies to another human being, Father. If you do, I'll tell everyone that *you* euthanized Mother. Then I'll deny everything."

"You're not human, Dev. We're finished. Please, just go." Milt was weary. If only he could drown in the bottle opposite him, he would. But he probably wouldn't have the courage for that either. He remained at his desk as Dev retreated from the room and left the house quietly. Then he laid his head in his hands and grieved again for Sophie, for Beatrice, for his son, for Shannon, for all of them and their sins that could never be forgiven.

Chapter Twenty-Seven

Lilly arrived at Milton Devon's at precisely seven the next morning. Her shift started in an hour, so she would have to be hasty. She needed his help.

She rang the doorbell of the old brownstone, only to be ignored. She'd seen Lucretia's sedan parked in the circular drive, so she expected to at least see the ebony-skinned maid come to the door.

Not easily deterred, Lilly rounded the side of the house to knock on the French patio doors. Lucretia was fixing breakfast and the frying bacon had drowned out the bell. She jumped when Lilly rapped on the glass. She looked immediately suspicious. Dr. Devon, Sr. wouldn't take kindly to an early morning solicitor, but then the heavy girl sure looked as if she was dressed in scrubs, like a nurse.

"Can I help you?" Lucretia opened the door just far enough to put herself between Lilly and the rest of the house.

"Could I please speak to Dr. Devon? He'll be expecting me."

"It's very early in the morning to be calling on the old doctor. I've just barely arrived myself. I haven't checked in with him yet."

"He and I are old friends and I'm taking care of his daughter-in-law, Shannon. If you will only let me in, I promise to be gentle. I know it's early."

Lilly knew she had won her over when she offered to

take Dr. Devon's first cup of coffee to him as well.

"I believe he's in the study already."

Lilly followed Lucretia to the heavy double-paneled doors of the study and then winked and waved, dismissing her before she popped inside to surprise Milt.

The scene before her sprang the nurse in her to action. Milt was lying with his head lolled strangely sideways on the desk. His skin was ashen, his lips pasty. She immediately set the coffee down and rushed over to him.

He was breathing, thank God. The stench of scotch floating from the pores and orifices of his body nearly knocked her over. The bottle was empty, as was the tumbler next to it. She noticed another tumbler across the desk that had liquid left in it. So he'd had a visitor.

Milt was hungover and she had half a mind, instead of waking him up and offering him the hot cup of coffee, to dump it over his head instead. She needed his *help* today. Of all times for him to get stinking drunk!

"Milton Devon!" She shook him with all of her might. "Milt! You will wake up now! I do not have time to deal with this!"

"What?" He was groggy, but definitely conscious. "I didn't drink that much, Sophie. Really."

"Well, obviously you did, Milt, because Sophie's been dead for years."

"Who the heck?" Milt rose from the desk, his hair plastered to the side that had lain there most of the night. He stared hard at Lilly, as if to place her.

"Oh, Lillian. It's you. I had quite forgotten your, uh, appearance."

She bit back a laugh. He still couldn't bring himself to mention her obvious weight gain. She was tired of hauling

187

around the fat suit, too.

"Coffee. You need three or four cups, immediately, Milt. And we need to talk while you're drinking them."

"Oh, Lillian, dear. I'm beyond help. I had hoped to actually poison myself on that bottle of scotch over there. By the throbbing in my brain and the steel wool in my throat, I can tell that I at least came close."

"Why in the world would you do that? We're just starting to make progress with Shannon."

"Beatrice is safe, Lillian. I sent her home."

"Oh. That's a relief, at least, but we still need to fix the problem of her mother."

"I told Dev that I'd told her everything. He unloaded on me, Lillian. I told you I would never disclose the extent of his indiscretions, but even I didn't realize the depths he'd sunk to."

"Can you tell me?"

Milt's eyes grew moist again as he thought of the conversation from the night before. "He took Sophie—first every ounce of respect she ever had for me, then he took her away from this world."

"He killed his own mother?" Lilly couldn't believe that Dev would have harmed Sophie. He adored her.

"It was what she wanted. He assisted her passing, sooner than it would have happened on its own. She was gravely ill. I didn't have the courage to let her go."

"Nor did you have the legal right to," Lilly replied. "You can't believe that he was right to do it."

"No, I don't agree with what he did, nor have I agreed with many of the things he's done over the years. But, you see, my silence has bid my approval. I'm going to Hell for sure."

"I know the way to salvation for you, Milt."

"I'm not sure I believe in it, but I'm listening."

"Shannon is healing, miraculously. She's talking and socializing and *remembering*. I'm thrilled for her and I'm terrified that the staff is going to report this back to Dev. I've warned her that it would be very dangerous for Dev to know, but it's getting increasingly difficult to hide her progress. She's even hiding her own medication. Remember that plant I mentioned? It's flourishing."

"I'm happy to hear that, Lillian, but what do you want *me* to do? Dev is her attending physician."

"I've learned that the medical advisory board will do an independent patient evaluation at the request of a member of a patient's immediate family. Apparently they stipulated this after hearing of doctor/family conspiracies keeping patients committed beyond what was required.

"Shannon can be evaluated by the medical board without Dev's knowledge if her immediate family member petitions to have the evaluation. You are her father-in-law. If you demanded that evaluation, with your reputation, I'm sure they'd comply immediately."

"Is it time for you to come out of disguise and make the request as her sister? The two of you could just leave after the evaluation is finished and your problem would be solved."

"Two small troubles with that theory: One, I'm a wanted fugitive and the statute of limitations never runs out on kidnapping, especially when the kidnapper has crossed state lines, which I did. Two, there would never be anywhere Shannon and I could hide from Dev, at least not forever, especially if he kept tabs on Beatrice."

"You're right. This is going to be my responsibility,

isn't it?"

"You have this chance to redeem yourself, Milt. You helped us all of those years ago and I will be forever grateful for that. But we need to end this. Shannon and I will leave after I've gotten her away from the hospital, but first we have to take care of Dev, so he can stop hurting all of us."

"What are you proposing, Lillian?"

"Just that we use the element of surprise to give the good doctor a taste of his own medicine."

"I will help you with Shannon. If she has made as much progress as you say, she will be a free woman before the end of the week. But I will not be a party to hurting my son. Even after all he's done, I cannot see fit to orphan Benjamin."

"Just help me with Shannon. I will take care of the rest. And you will never need to worry about Benjamin. I'll take care of him too."

"From your mouth to the Good Lord's ears, Lillian. We're going to need all the help we can get."

CHAPTER TWENTY-EIGHT

Dev was showering, cleaning away the last traces of his overnight tryst. His loins tingled, grateful for the release he'd allowed himself for the first time in several weeks. The redhead had been very intense, young, willing, and he'd taken her wantonly, repeatedly.

He groaned as he realized how short-lived the pleasure always was, for he had to make sure that the woman discreetly left before Benjamin arrived home from his Friday night movie night. He went through the haste of giving the girl a false phone number and assuring her that he would call later, tossing her number carelessly to the foyer waste basket as she left shyly through the front door, her face full of promise.

It was a performance repeated often, with little variation. When his needs got the best of him, he would go to a mall restaurant lounge or a hip nightspot and watch for someone young and opportunistic. He wanted someone who would go home with a single, successful doctor (for he always removed his wedding ring on nights like these,) and hope to earn a meal ticket in exchange for a night in his bed. Their hopes would never be realized, he knew, but the pleasure would be mutual, at least while it lasted.

It was meaningless. His heart did and always would belong to Shannon. He'd cared somewhat for Diana because she'd given him a son, but he'd also learned from her that he should never again get involved with somebody from work. After all, like any hospital, rumors traveled at St. Louis State. His conquests would never link him to the place he was most revered. They knew where he lived, but shame never, ever brought anyone back to his door.

He dressed in a burgundy cashmere wool sweater with a white undershirt and gray wool slacks. He combed his white blond hair thoughtfully to the side and dabbed on a trace of Shannon's favorite cologne. Examining himself, he decided he looked rather young for his fifty-three years. His dark eyes were still minimally lined and he had good, strong teeth. Shannon and he would make a beautiful couple again when she got well.

He hadn't seen her all week and he fairly hummed with anticipation. He wondered if his withdrawal of the medication was beginning to make a difference. So far, his staff had not reported any major changes.

He had thought intensely about his next move after his visit with his father. Beatrice was gone now. There was a way to make things right, but in order to put his plans to action, it would be necessary to re-alter Shannon's condition.

He was already well on his way to gaining a post at the University of Washington hospital in Seattle. They'd taken his *circum vitae* with all of the enthusiasm he'd expected and Dev had already contacted a realtor and the administration at Seattle Preparatory Academy, for Benjamin. He'd spent much of Thursday and Friday working out the details. They would be moving to Seattle within the span of a month.

If Beatrice wouldn't stay close to him, then he was determined to be closer to her. She would be starting school at the University soon. After hearing his father's version of the truth, Dev was positive that their reunion would be stilted, at best, but he was confident that he could win her over.

Dev was taking control. It made him angry that all of his actions—what his father deemed unforgivable—were purely reactionary. He'd been denied pleasure by his wife, so his reaction was to take a lover. She'd gotten pregnant, so he'd taken in their son. His wife had objected, so he'd forced her to agree. Then his daughter had been kidnapped—that he'd been unable to react to, until now.

He was not going to lose her again. He could have it all. He just simply needed Shannon to sail through the admissions process to the Seattle long-term care unit.

He'd already drawn up the syringe of *Risperidone* and put it in the inside pocket of his matching blazer. It was time to pay his lovely wife a Saturday visit as he had so many times over the years. He slipped his platinum wedding band onto his left hand and straightened his mussed bed on his way through his suite. Carlotta would change the sheets later, as she always did at the start of the weekend.

Dev whistled as he jingled his keys in rhythm on his way to his car. Everything would work out perfectly. He would see to it.

He stopped at the corner flower market on his way from the parking garage to the hospital. Shannon had loved St. Louis for its wide array of orchids, more varieties than any other place in the States. They were her favorite flower. He bought a large bouquet, wrapped in lavender tulle and cellophane, for she loved purple also.

He could hide the injection of her medication behind the huge bouquet. Not that anyone would be watching that closely, but he tried to be discreet. There was no sense in risking discovery.

Dev stopped at the nurse's station to review Shannon's chart, asking a diminutive nurse's aide to hold the bunch of flowers. He smiled charmingly at her as he sought out his wife's record. Why, the flowers were almost as big as she was!

Dev was in a jolly mood, but it dissipated as he turned the carousel of charts and found his wife's out of its usual place. Who else would have been looking at it that day? The nurse, whoever she was, was going to pay the piper for misplacing it. Dev's expression grew increasingly sour as he found nobody at the nurse's station who could explain where the missing paperwork had gone.

He asked for the charge nurse for the shift. He was greeted by a stout young man with a black goatee and ceil blue hospital scrubs.

"We haven't met. I'm Dr. Dev Devon and my wife is in room four hundred fifty-one. Her chart has been misplaced and I demand to know what's happened to it."

"I'm Carl Rupert, the charge nurse. It's nice to meet you, Dr. Devon. I'd been told that you might visit today by yesterday's charge, Darcy."

"I realize that the hospital is trying to make most records electronic, but it is widely known that I've preferred to still have a tangible version of my wife's own chart. I've kept them coinciding for some time now. Do you know where it might have gone?"

"To my knowledge, the paperwork is making its way to medical records to be filed away."

"You mean they've decided to defy my wishes regarding the paper record? Without consulting me?"

The young man shifted, uncomfortably, clearly bothered by the angry doctor confronting him.

"I mean that the chart of every patient who is discharged gets routed to medical records to be scanned into a permanent electronic record."

Dev's neck grew hot. Why had he worn a blasted wool sweater? He hated to sweat. His voice grew quieter, more lethal.

"Perhaps I misunderstood. You mentioned discharge as the reason for moving a chart. Are you trying to tell me that my wife has been *discharged*, without my knowledge?"

"I'm afraid so, Sir. She left yesterday."

"She *left*? She's a committed inpatient. I am her primary provider. There is no way she could just walk out of here."

"Her care was transferred to another provider by the medical review board at the request of her family."

"What *family*?" Dev could only think of two people who might achieve such a thing—his father or Lillian. Either one of them had made a huge mistake, thinking he would leave this situation gracefully.

"I'm afraid I've told you all that I can. The patient is no longer in your care, so I can't share any other information with you because of privacy laws."

Dev was in the young man's face in an instant, but another staff nurse had seen the problem developing and she had called security. He had alerted the administrator, who had been standing by, aware that a situation could arise from the discharge of Mrs. Devon.

He knew that the board had not only found Shannon

Devon competent for discharge, they had found, through her new provider's toxicology tests, that she was recovering from doses of a neuroleptic agent that was not on her chart, *Risperidone.*

Dr. Milton Devon, Junior, was officially under investigation by the hospital board and the local police. He was suspected of illegally obtaining and drugging his wife with a substance that had kept her wrongfully hospitalized for seventeen years. The problem was, the administrator knew, that Dev Devon wasn't aware of these events, which had taken place Thursday and Friday.

Security was on hand as Dev was temporarily relieved of his hospital privileges and escorted to his office to take any belongings he wished to possess before they changed the locks pursuant to the investigation. His visit to the office was supervised. Much to Dev's horror, he wasn't able to pocket the vials of *Risperidone* he had stowed in the bottom drawer of his desk.

His mind was so befuddled, that he wasn't able to think of much he would actually need from his office, except his humidor of expensive Cuban cigars and a full bottle of the scotch his father had given him. He put these and his Rolodex into a file box that the administrator had already placed in the center of his desk. At the last moment, he grabbed his photos of Shannon, Beatrice, and Benjamin and placed them carefully on top of the other contents.

Dev was then numbly escorted from the place where he'd begun his illustrious, and until now, unblemished career. It took closing his car door in the off-campus garage to jar him into realizing that he was cornered. Grief struck him for a moment and he grimaced with the pain of it.

But then good, clean anger took its place. His career

might be ruined, but Dev would never go quietly. He would get to the bottom of this. He would find Shannon and they would be a family again.

CHAPTER TWENTY-NINE

Extracting Shannon from the clutches of her prison had been surprisingly, mercifully easy. Dr. Milton Devon, Senior, had used every ounce of wherewithal to insure that her exit was irreproachable. Her freedom would come at a huge price to his son. He wanted to make sure it would stick.

That the medical board and the authorities were investigating Dev for criminal misconduct was nothing to do with Milt's part in getting Shannon discharged. They had deduced his malpractice through their own means. Still, he knew that Dev would soon be at his doorstep, anxious to punish him further.

But Milt had done as he had said he would do. He had gotten Shannon out and he had given her over to her sister. He had never learned the whereabouts of Lillian's home, so he didn't know where they had gone. He secretly hoped they would simply flee and Dev would be left to wonder forever of their location. Lillian had done it once before. She could do it again.

What about Beatrice, though? She wouldn't be able to hide and Lillian knew this. Beatrice would never be party to the kind of deception she now detested. Plus, she would never leave the friendships behind that he knew fortified her and gave her the courage to find her past in the first place.

If Lillian and Shannon wanted to be part of Beatrice's

life, they would have to find another way to deal with Dev. He was slippery enough and had a clean enough record to escape jail. There would have to be some other way.

Milt wanted nothing to do with it, any of it.

So he worked in his yard that Saturday, putting thoughts of his family aside. He thought only of dahlia bulbs and coffee grounds and cultivation of the soil. He thought of the miniature orchid gardens he should like to surround his aging oak trees with in the spring. He contemplated which sort of landscape lighting he would prefer to light variegated ivy along his circular front drive.

Milt thought forward to the Sunday dinner he'd planned with Benjamin. He and the boy hadn't visited in a while. He'd seen the local tennis standings in the paper. His grandson was doing him proud, yet again.

He would have Lucretia make her famous beef stew and Southern corn bread. It was Benjamin's favorite. Milt always enjoyed their visits immensely. His grandson was cut from the same cloth he was. He loved a good debate and action movies. Benjamin was athletic and loved the outdoors, like Milt always had. They'd understood each other and they were closer than Benjamin and Dev ever were.

Milt was wrapped up in thoughts of his son and grandson, setting more mulch about the azaleas close to the fence line in the back yard. He was humming a Nat King Cole tune under his breath. He never even heard the muted footsteps in the grass behind him. Nor did he feel anything after the quick jolt of the small-caliber bullet lodging in his brain. He was dead before his face hit the soil in front of him.

The police would later suspect a robbery. Lucretia

had arrived at the house Saturday afternoon, to find the front door wide open and the house completely disheveled. Every drawer and file and cabinet had been pulled open and emptied. Jewelry boxes were cleared of their contents and expensive paintings removed from the walls. Most of the crystal had been smashed and the study reeked of liquor from the obliterated carafes that Milt had always kept stocked.

The gun was lying neatly on the desk calendar, pearl-handled, just 38-caliber. Lucretia recognized it as Dr. Devon's. It, of course, dusted clean for fingerprints.

Lucretia had found Milt himself, lying facedown in his beloved flowerbed and she had been able to do nothing for him but to close his eyes, wipe the grime from his face, and cry for him.

Forever unexplained was the appearance of priceless paintings at the back door of the Art History Museum and the irreplaceable jewels that had made their way to the bottom of a fountain in Forest Park. The link between these and the tragic death of Milton Devon, Sr. was never made. The finders simply thanked their lucky stars and the world kept on turning, less one fine, older gentleman.

CHAPTER THIRTY

Dev had expected to find Shannon at his father's home. At the very least, he expected that Milt would have arranged her travel and given her the funds to make her escape as he had for Beatrice. It was with huge frustration that he rifled through his father's house and found no trace of Shannon's whereabouts.

He was sure that Milt was guilty of helping Shannon, because Lillian could never have gotten past the hospital's security process. It was widely known that she'd kidnapped Dr. Dev Devon's daughter.

It was the certain knowledge that his father had let him down once again that reassured Dev that his actions had been warranted. His father had finally gotten the treatment he deserved. Dev covered his tracks and left without looking back.

Lillian shed her disguise once she and Shannon were home on Friday night. Shannon was still confused at times and her speech was stilted, but she understood her surroundings. She knew that her sister had saved her, just as she had saved her daughter so many years before.

Minus her fat suit, wig, and colored contacts, Lillian looked like a slightly older version of the sister Shannon had always loved. Her honey-blond hair was cut short to accommodate the wig. It looked different, but her eyes returned to the dark violet that almost mirrored Shannon's own eyes. If anything, Lillian was slimmer than she'd been years ago.

They spent Saturday and Sunday getting reacquainted. Lilly knew there was no way Milt or Dev could locate her and she'd put her resignation in at the hospital before she'd checked out on Friday. She'd hated to disappoint Virginia by not giving notice, but it had been necessary. Without Milt's help, Dev could never link her to Darcy White and this address belonged to the woman by that name.

Shannon and Lilly were planning a life in relative obscurity on Bainbridge Island, a small island in Washington State just a ferry ride away from Seattle. They'd picked the location by its darkness on a nighttime satellite map and by its proximity to Beatrice. Lilly had her savings and the pending sale of her Pateros house to make their life comfortable there.

They would contact Beatrice eventually, but only after she was safe from Dev and his clutches.

Lilly had planned bodily harm to Dev and Shannon was supportive of whatever action she chose to take. The trouble was that she had promised Milt that she would protect Benjamin. Lilly wanted to exact revenge upon Dev for all he had taken away from her sister, but her instinct now was to flee and not fight and to let the poor, innocent byproduct of all of this mess, the boy, live the remainder of his childhood the way he always had.

Well, it might be a little different, because his father would be out of a job. That knowledge bolstered Lilly's mood. Ruining Dev's medical career had been a bonus. He could always sell his home or rely on his savings to keep Benjamin in school. But Dev wouldn't be able to hurt anybody else the way he had hurt Shannon.

Lilly made plans to leave the fourth week of September, before the first of the month rent on the apartment would be due. Internet access allowed she and Shannon to make their plans from afar. Lilly toyed with the idea of opening another bakery in an empty storefront somewhere. The realtor they communicated with had a place in mind that had an apartment on the second floor. She could cover the rent, but she would need capital to buy the equipment they needed to get started.

Milt had basically told them to get lost and not come back, but he had alluded to Lilly that should she need help with anything—expenses, travel, whatever—that she should call him. He would help, like he had before. Lilly saw an opportunity in opening this new business and it took her mind off of the man she most wanted to hurt. Couldn't success be a deterrent, a way to make a clean break without feeling like an end was left untied?

Lilly resolved to call Milt on Tuesday. It would be the last time she would ask for his help. Dev would only hurt him more if he knew Milt was involved with her and Shannon. When Milt didn't answer the phone all day or night, Lilly decided she would go to the house to check on him.

She donned her disguise the next morning and rang the front bell. She peeked in the foyer window. That was when she saw the police tape stretched across the inside of the house. Lilly walked to the nearest neighboring house and rang the bell.

Another older, distinguished gentleman answered the door.

"Excuse me, Sir. I'm sorry to bother you, but I can't

seem to reach your neighbor next door. I noticed the police markings and I'm wondering if you might know what happened there."

"Unfortunately, young lady, I do. The disturbance was pretty hard to ignore. Made me afraid for my own safety, I'll tell you that."

Lilly waited for him to continue.

"That poor man never bothered anybody and his gardens were fit for a city park. He and his wife and my wife and I were friends years ago. We're both widowed and we talked over the fence once in a while."

"What happened to him?"

"He was robbed. Shot in the head while he was working outside. I'll never understand why they couldn't just knock him out or something. Why'd they have to kill him?"

Lilly's blood ran cold. She knew in her gut exactly why Milt had been murdered in cold blood. She also knew that a robbery was the least likely reason. Dev Devon was responsible. He had delivered to his father the ultimate punishment.

She was visibly upset and the man reached for her arm, seeking to steady her.

Lilly automatically backed away. "I'm sorry I disturbed you. I need to leave now. Thank you for the information."

With that, Lilly abruptly left. She took several deep gulps of air when she returned to her car. Dev was dangerous, beyond what even she'd imagined. She could never carry out her plan, because Dev would forever be on the hunt for Shannon and for her, and for Beatrice. She cried for the thousandth time for everything he'd taken from them and for the first time for her dear friend, Milt.

CHAPTER THIRTY-ONE

Dev tried to go on as usual, primarily so that Benjamin wouldn't be privy to the fact that he'd been suspended at work. They met at the country club often for dinner. Dev spent much of his daytime poring over legal volumes, learning the ins and outs of malpractice and wrongful investigation by medical boards.

He was finagling a way to make his late father the guilty party, trying to pin any misdeeds on him and his advanced age and history of poor judgment.

Benjamin was taking his grandfather's death unexpectedly hard. Dev understood that for any family member of a murder victim, the hardest part was dealing with suddenness and the senselessness of the crime. Benjamin was angry with the culprit, breathlessly so. He wanted to see the proper people punished. He also refused to hear of his father selling the house or any of his grandfather's things.

Benjamin, with the rationality of the teenager that he was, wanted everything to remain the same. And eventually, he wanted to live in his grandfather's lovely old house. Dev had never understood Benjamin's attachment to the old man, but then his son didn't know what a louse Milt had been. Keeping the house was out of the question. He would sell it as soon as possible.

Benjamin needn't know this, though. Like most subjects they disagreed about, Dev would simply do what he wanted and disappoint his son later. Benjamin always got over it.

The other subject his son just couldn't seem to get past was moving to Seattle. He had gotten to know Beatrice well enough to be glad for her that she had made her choice and it was making her happy. She was keeping in touch with him on his cell phone, unbeknownst to Dev.

She would be horrified if the two of them just showed up and insinuated themselves back into her life. It wasn't that she wanted to never see Benjamin again. She just explained that there were things about their father that unsettled her, without explaining what those things were. She most definitely did not want to see Dev anytime soon.

It was a Saturday night and Benjamin was going out with his friends to check out a new under-eighteen nightspot. He'd spiked his hair into the proper amount of dishevelment and sprayed it into place. He'd dressed to kill in Diesel jeans, a dark blue button-down oxford with a black t-shirt underneath, and black Kenneth Cole tie-up ankle boots.

He looked like he'd stepped out of a teen magazine when he came bounding out the door to his friend's already packed silver Isuzu. He never even noticed that the door didn't shut behind him or that two slim shadowed figures slipped quietly into his home. He was out and he was having fun.

The inside of the house was too quiet for Dev. He and Benjamin had always lived like this and since Benjamin had hit his teen years, Dev often had the house to himself. But Beatrice's light had changed all that. She'd brought new energy to the large old home and Dev felt unexpectedly lonely when he was solo, as he was tonight.

It made him glad he'd decided to finally sell the huge old place. The only thing he would miss was his bedroom suite. As he prepared a small meal of tossed salad and toast, Dev anticipated sitting in his cozy recliner and watching an old movie from the home theater. After dinner, he would allow himself a martini with two olives and perhaps a brandy nightcap. He wouldn't stay up too late because Benjamin felt it unnecessary for him to wait up.

He was carrying his plate and a full glass of milk and tucked the latter into the crook of his arm as he opened his bedroom suite door. The scene before him took him completely by surprise. He nearly dropped both of the dishes in the haste to set them aside.

Shannon was dressed in a navy blue pantsuit, perfectly color coordinated with the settee on which she perched. Her honey-blond hair flowed around her shoulders and her eyes sparkled in anticipation. She had come back to him and she was a vision.

"Shannon? Am I dreaming, darling? I thought, no, I feared that I would never see you again in this place that we made together."

"It's still beautiful."

It was heaven to hear her speak, even though the sentence was slightly broken and spoken with obvious effort. And she was looking at him, into his eyes. He hadn't seen her like this in years. It nearly broke his heart.

"You're beautiful too, Shannon. I've missed you more than you know."

She rose and crossed to him. He was mesmerized as she grabbed his hand and led him deeper into the darkened bedroom. Just one sconce was lit between the bed and entertainment center. She turned at the end of the bed and

208

grasped his free hand. His back was to the dressing room door behind him.

Shannon gazed deeply into his eyes and she touched his face. He was unable to contain himself any longer. He'd wanted her for so long and now his every desire was coming true. He leaned forward to kiss her.

And then he felt a needle stab into the exposed flesh of his neck. He grabbed for it in surprise and pain, but the plunger had already been depressed. Even as he was extracting it and whirling toward the slight figure of his long-lost sister-in-law, who had impaled him, the air that had been injected violently and directly into his carotid artery was embolizing rapidly into the corners of his brain.

Dev was having a stroke. First to disappear was his speech. He wanted to ask why these women had done this to him, but he already knew deep inside that he'd hurt them irreversibly, even this woman who he had once loved so much.

His arms and legs grew numb and could no longer hold him, so he slumped to the floor. His fingers twitched and Lillian quickly retrieved the spent needle from his reach. No sense taking chances. Dev's eyes lost focus and as he stared vacantly ahead, Lillian thought what a sweet thing justice could be.

When he was still, she cleaned the blood away from his wound with an alcohol swab. The prick wasn't terribly evident. Dev was still breathing, as he would be when Benjamin found him the next morning after he didn't arrive as usual for Sunday brunch. They paid little attention as the weary women walked away at last from Dr. Dev Devon.

EPILOGUE

Doctors would try in vain to undo the damage to
Dev's brain. They marveled at how tragic it was that such
a brilliant medical mind should be trapped into a body that
breathed, but would no longer do the mind's bidding. Dev
would have to spend the remainder of his life in a nursing
home.

Benjamin was upset by his father's sudden illness, but
then the news filtered to him that his father had been under
investigation for drugging Shannon Devon. Beatrice filled
him in on the rest of his father's behavior and Benjamin
found himself suddenly hating the man who had hurt so
many people for so many years.

Benjamin missed his grandfather because he knew that
Milt understood the extent of Dev's transgressions and he
would have been sympathetic.

As it was, there really was no one to turn to. Benjamin
found himself needing to make adult decisions, facing
two estates that would need disassembled and attended to.
The State of Missouri recognized him as a minor without
adult supervision and they were making arrangements to
put Benjamin into foster care until he reached the age of
eighteen.

Then one day, about a week after his father's stroke, he
found himself facing Shannon Devon in his father's sitting
room. She had appealed to his caseworker to have him
placed into her care. After careful psychiatric assessment,

they had found her competent to act as Benjamin's guardian. He marveled at her generosity. After all, he now knew that she'd been forced all of these years to act as his mother, when she'd had nothing to do with his parentage.

Shannon and Lillian couldn't bring themselves to leave for Washington without Beatrice's now-beloved brother. He was a good kid and he didn't deserve the fallout of Dev's actions. They would see that he finished high school and they would guide him through the probate of his grandfather's estate and the downsizing of his father's. They would all live at Milt's until June, when Benjamin would graduate and pursue his tennis career, something he looked eagerly forward to.

Bree had a tearful reunion with Lilly the day before she was to leave for Seattle. Lilly had gone straight from Dev's to her apartment with Shannon and to the airport. She and Bree had anticipated the day she would leave for college since the start of her senior year. Lilly was now free to see her niece off from Pateros and that she did.

It was a bittersweet reunion with Penny and the Pakootas family. Penny was overjoyed that Lilly was out of trouble and that she would be free to return to them, but she was still hurt that her dear friend had never shared her mysterious past. They would have lots of time to talk about why, though, because Penny insisted on selling the bakery back so that Lilly could return to Pateros.

Lilly wouldn't agree to buy the bakery, but she did agree to become equal partners with Penny. It was what they both deserved, since Penny had put as much heart into the business as Lilly had. Shannon would be accepted into the fold as a clerk, and once she learned to drive again, a delivery person. It would all be arranged from afar so that when they returned in June, the bakery could accommodate them all.

Lilly took her house back off the market and saw that Bree's things were delivered to her in Seattle from storage. She would rent the home over the next nine months, since housing was at a premium in the small town of Pateros. Then she and Shannon would move back in with Bree in time for her freshman summer break.

None of them would have to worry about money since her half of the two Devon estates afforded Bree more funds than she would ever spend on her own.

Bree and Nonnie and Asher were tighter than ever. Lilly was surprised to discover that a romance had blossomed between Bree and Asher. Bree had never had much time for dating, so it was actually fun to see them so sweet on each other. Lilly left again for St. Louis after the four had parted with the promise of the coming year on all of their minds.

Nonnie would go to school in San Francisco and get her first culinary job as a sous chef at an eatery at Pike Place Market in Seattle. She and Bree were inseparable once again. Asher would spend his first year at Eastern Washington University and transfer for his final two years and a Master's Degree in Education from the University of Washington.

Benjamin's professional tennis career would lead him frequently to the West Coast, where the entire family would travel to watch his summer tournaments.

They would all emerge from the lies of their early lives not unscathed, but unbroken, free at last from the clutches of deceit. Life was sweet and it would go on with the lightest of steps and only the deepest depths of honesty for BreeAnn and all of the people she loved.

About The Author

Kimberly Ann Freel

Kimberly Ann Freel was born and raised in rural Okanogan County, Washington, where she still resides with her husband and four children.

She is an avid reader and enjoys cooking, gardening, and spending time with her close family.

This is her second novel.

Don't Miss

Painted Rocks: A Novel

By Kimberly Ann Freel

Inspirational and heart-wrenching, *Painted Rocks*
is a story for anyone who has ever gone to lengths to
conceal the past, only to find that it can never really
be laid to rest.

*Available in Paperback from
CMP Publishing at cmppg.com
or at Amazon.com.*

Made in the USA